Books by Layne Walker are available at
amazon.com and other online stores

Action Adventure Novels
Escaping Yellowstone

Fantasy Adventure Novels
Tainted Gold
Convergence of Time

Young Adult Adventure
Time Hackers

Short Story Collection
Gold Balls of Fur and Other Snapshots of Life

Go to
www.laynewalkerbooks.com
for a preview of Lavne's next book.

GW00689583

Escaping Yellowstone

Layne Walker

Wild Mustangs Publishing, LLC

Escaping Yellowstone

ISBN-13: 978-0615612386

Published by
Wild Mustangs Publishing, LLC
Lake Havasu City, AZ

Visit Layne's website at
www.laynewalkerbooks.com

Printing history
First edition published in 2012

Dedication

Many heartfelt thanks to Anne Cote.
You got me started on this exciting, challenging,
and sometimes frustrating journey of becoming a
writer.
I'm honored to have someone as
loving, patient, and understanding
as you by my side.

Special thanks to Anita Batz
for putting up with me for the last year.

I also want to thank Ellen Brunio.
Your kind words of encouragement were, and still
are, greatly appreciated.

Part I

The Eruption

Chapter 1

Sam Jones sat in his recliner in Buffalo, Wyoming, watching *Fox News* out of Cheyenne. He thought about all the 2012 hoopla that had been going on for the last year, and how it reminded him of the scare of 2000, when everybody thought computers would crash. Well, here it was, Friday evening, December 21, 2012, and nothing had happened. "What a joke," he muttered, "all that worrying . . . for what? Nothing, not even a cosmic fart." He chuckled.

He got up out of his easy chair and started for the kitchen to get another beer. Stopping, he cocked his head to one side and listened. It sounded like a train, headed towards the house. The sound grew louder with every passing second. He felt his eyes bulging, and his heart began to race as he realized it wasn't a train, but an earthquake.

The next thing he knew, he was flying across the room, landing on an antique table his wife had bought two years earlier in Vermont. "Oh, shit," he cried out as he crashed into the 200-year-old table. He tried to stand up, but the house shook so violently, he was thrown back on the floor.

Thinking about his wife and two kids, Dave and Ashley, he panicked. "Linda, Linda," he called. She had been in the kitchen starting dinner the last time he had seen her. Ashley had gone to her friend Jenny's house for the night. Dave was somewhere upstairs.

He tried to crawl across the floor, but the house still bucked violently. "Dammit," he yelled as he lunged off the floor in an attempt to get to the kitchen. The china hutch, sitting next to the kitchen door, came crashing down, barely missing him, shooting pieces of glass and china across the room like tiny missiles. A cloud of dust billowed up, stinging his eyes and making it hard to breathe. He crawled through the debris, wiping at his eyes with the sleeve of his shirt.

Then, just as suddenly as it had started, the earthquake stopped. The lights had gone out. The house creaked in the eerie silence.

"Linda, where are you?" he yelled, pulling himself up with the door jamb. The late afternoon sunlight filtered through the kitchen window.

"I'm under the table."

She stood up as he stumbled through the debris scattered across the floor. When he reached the table, he slipped and fell, hitting his head on the edge. "Son-of-a-bitch," he growled, standing up and rubbing the growing lump. He quickly looked over Linda. Under her mussed blond hair, her face contorted with fear. Her lips trembled. A wild, feral look haunted her eyes. He'd never seen her this terrified. "Are you okay?"

"No, I'm not okay," she spit. "I'm scared to death. I'm worried about my kids. I need to see if they're okay." She shoved her way past him.

Sam grabbed her arm. "I'm worried about the kids, too, but it's not safe. You could get hurt. Let me get them."

She slapped his hand away. "Leave me alone," she hissed. "I have to go."

They hadn't been getting along for some time, but they had always tolerated each other. He knew how stubborn she could be, but now, she seemed to be on the edge of losing control.

Before Sam could stop her, a strong aftershock hit,

rocking the house and knocking both of them to the floor. Linda let out an ear-piercing scream and Sam threw himself on top of her as the refrigerator doors flew open, spraying the contents of the fridge across the room, pelting both of them with food and liquids. He buried his face against Linda's neck as the floor bucked and swayed. He could feel dirt and debris falling on his back. He prayed to God that the house wouldn't collapse, or even worse, catch fire. He wondered how Dave was faring upstairs.

The aftershock lasted a few seconds. When it stopped, he rolled off Linda's back and slowly stood up.

As he tried to help her up, she jerked away, yelling, "Leave me alone. I need to find Dave and Ashley."

"Damnit, woman," Sam shot back with anger, gripping both her arms and shaking her lightly, "get yourself together. I'll go upstairs and get Dave. You stay here and get the emergency radio out of the pantry. We need to find out how bad the quake was."

"Dammit, Sam," she roared, "I don't care what kind of damage the quake did. I want my kids."

Trying to keep his temper in check, Sam took a deep breath. Still holding her, he said calmly, "We'll get the kids, but we need to find out how much damage the quake caused. In case you've forgotten, Ashley's at Jenny's house. If we're going to get her, I need to know how much damage the quake caused." He released her, then yanked open a drawer and grabbed three dish towels.

Linda pursed her lips in defiance, turned, and started for the door.

He grabbed her arm again and jerked her around. "I told you I would go, dammit," he snapped, "but I'm not going to sacrifice our safety in the process." Squeezing her arm, he glared at her, daring her to defy him again.

With tears streaming down her face, the fire left her

eyes. She nodded her head.

He released her and turned on the faucet to get the towels wet. The water dribbled to a stop. *The main underground pipe must have broken in the quake.* He walked to the mess that had spilled out of the fridge, got a bottle of water, and poured it over the towels. "Here, put this over your mouth and breathe through it. It'll keep you from breathing in all this dust."

She yanked the towel out of his hand and spun around, heading for the pantry.

He put the towel over his nose and mouth, then headed for the stairs. Carefully making his way through the living room and the debris scattered on the floor, he looked at the walls and ceiling, trying to gage how much damage the quake had done.

His grandfather had built the house on twenty acres in 1906, about ten miles south of Buffalo. After his dad had died, Sam inherited the property. Before moving in, he and Linda had gutted the house, completely remodeling it.

The house had been solidly built and, as far as Sam could tell now, it didn't look like there had been too much damage. A couple of cracks showed in the plaster on the walls. Some of the windows had shattered. Otherwise, it looked like the house had come through pretty much intact.

He had only taken three steps up the stairs when the staircase loudly cracked and fell an inch. He grabbed the hand rail as his heart jumped to his throat. He hoped the stairs wouldn't collapse under his weight. Carefully, he continued his way up, one step at a time. At the top, he let out a sigh of relief, only then realizing he had been holding his breath.

Dave's door frame had twisted. The door wouldn't open.

Sam put his shoulder to the door and threw his 160 pounds against it to force it open. Peering through the haze of dust filling the room, he saw the quake had tipped over the wooden bunk beds. He couldn't see Dave. "Dave," he yelled. "Dave . . . where are you?"

"Dad, thank God you're here. I'm trapped under the bunk beds."

Drawing closer, Sam saw Dave lying on the floor between the upper and lower bunks. He rushed across the room. "Are you okay?"

"Yeah, but my legs are stuck. I can't get enough leverage to get the beds off me." Dave lay on his stomach with the bed covering him from the waist down.

Gripping the frame, Sam lifted it until Dave pulled his legs free. "Are you sure you're okay?"

Dave stood up and rubbed his legs. "I'm fine, just a little bruised. What about you and Mom? Are you two okay?"

"Your mom's fine. I'm a little banged up, but I'll live." Sam held out the wet towel. "Here, put this over your nose and mouth, so you won't be breathing in all this dust."

Dave took it and tied it in place it over his lower face. "What happened? Was it an earthquake?"

"I'm pretty sure it was, but I'm not positive. Your mom has the emergency radio on downstairs. Let's go see if she's heard anything yet."

At the top of the stairs, he turned to Dave. "Walk lightly when you go down. The steps were damaged and I'm not sure how much weight they can take. I'll wait here until you get to the bottom, then I'll come down."

As Dave carefully made his way down the stairs, Sam watched and listened for signs that the staircase wouldn't be able to support Dave's weight. Even though he was only seventeen, at six-foot-two, he was six inches taller than Sam, and he weighed a solid 190 pounds. The stairs creaked and moaned, but held up.

As Sam cautiously made his way down, his mind raced ahead. *I need to call Jenny's dad and find out if Ashley's okay. That is, if my cell phone still works. If not, I'll drive the four-wheeler to get her.*

As Sam walked into the kitchen, he saw Linda sitting on the floor with her head in her hands, rocking back and forth, saying, "No, no, no," over and over.

Fearing she'd been hurt, he rushed to her. "What's wrong? Are you okay?"

Looking up, tears running down her face, she whispered, "Yellowstone."

Puzzled, he asked, "Yellowstone? What about Yellowstone?"

"Yellowstone exploded."

"What do you mean 'Yellowstone exploded'?"

"The radio said Yellowstone exploded."

"Dave, get the radio and see if you can figure out what she's talking about." He wiped the tears off of her face and realized she was in shock. *My God, what's going on? Is this a delayed reaction to the quake? Shit, this is all I need right now.*

Dave picked the radio off of the floor and turned up the volume as Sam helped Linda get into a chair.

" . . . say it is the worst sight they have ever seen," said the voice on the radio. "Once again, this is Mark Pratt of KBUF radio in Buffalo with breaking news. It seems that the super-volcano underneath Yellowstone National Park has erupted. We don't have many details yet, but we have been in contact with people by cell phone who are in Cody, and they are saying that this is the real deal folks."

Sam and Dave looked at each other, too stunned at the news to talk.

"Witnesses say that the ash cloud is already at least two miles high and getting higher all the time. Uh, oh, . . . wait a minute, I've just been handed an update. This is from the governor's office. Okay, this says that, even though it seems that the volcano has erupted, it hasn't been confirmed yet. They don't want anyone to panic. You are all to remain where you are and wait for further instructions."

Dave turned the volume down. "If the volcano did erupt, we need to get out of here as soon as possible. We talked about this in geography class. My teacher said that, if the Yellowstone volcano erupted, the ash cloud would cover this area within hours, and anyone still here would be buried alive."

Sam wasn't completely sure the volcano had erupted, and he didn't want to make a foolish decision or go running off without having all the facts. "We don't know that the volcano erupted for sure. Maybe it was just a really big earthquake, and what they think is an ash cloud is really just dust. Let's listen to the radio and see what else they have to say."

Sam reached over and turned up the volume. He wanted to find out what had really happened, then he would go get Ashley.

" . . . am on the phone with Nancy," said the newscaster, "who lives in Greybull. Nancy, can you tell us what you see?"

"Well, we live on the west side of Greybull, in a beautiful Tudor home, on five acres, with a beautiful view to the west and— "

"Nancy, I'm sorry to interrupt you. I'm sure you have a nice house, but could you just tell us what you can see?"

"Oh, yes, I'm sorry. Well, I'm on my patio looking to the west and, even though it's almost dusk, I can see a huge cloud rising up in the . . . oh, my God! No! No! Noooo!"

"Nancy . . . Nancy. . . . Well, we seem to have lost reception with Nancy. I hope she's okay. Let's move on to Mike. Mike, are you there?"

"Yes, Mark, I'm here."

"Okay, Mike, where are you and what can you tell us?"

"First of all, I'm with the National Volcano Research Foundation, and I want to go on record here and say that I disagree with the statement from the government that you just read. The volcano did erupt, and everybody within four hundred miles in any direction of ground-zero needs to evacuate immediately. Within the initial blast zone, which we expect to be around fifty miles, nothing will survive. Anyone or anything that close is already dead. After the ash cloud gets beyond there, it will slow down to approximately fifty- or sixty-miles-per-hour, and will fan out in every direction. We estimate it will hit Buffalo in a little over one hour and will dump at least four to five feet of ash over the next few days. And it's not just the ash that you have to worry about . . . this cloud also contains toxic gasses. Even if you cover your face, you're not going to be safe unless you wear a gas mask."

Sam's mind was working overtime, trying to process the information he was hearing. It didn't seem possible to him that the volcano had really erupted, or that they were in danger of being buried alive or asphyxiated by toxic gasses. He looked at Linda, who was still rocking back and forth. The earthquake had upset her pretty badly and, now, to hear this must have been too much for her mind to handle.

Dave turned the radio off and heavily sat down on a chair. "What are we going to do now, Dad?"

Sam felt torn. On the one hand, he wanted to get

Ashley and make sure she was okay. On the other, if he took the time to go get her and bring her back, the ash cloud and toxic gasses might overtake them before they could get out of town.

He turned to Dave as he made his decision. "We need to get out of here as quickly as we can. You throw some blankets and sleeping bags in the truck. In fact, let's throw in all the camping gear. If we have to camp out, we'll be glad we brought it. I'm going to grab the guns and ammo, and maybe the bow and arrows. After you pack the camping stuff, grab some food, nothing perishable, canned stuff. Oh, and clothes, lots of warm clothes: coats, hats, gloves. It's not snowing right now, but I don't know what the weather's going to be like for the next few days. If you can think of anything else we may need, throw it in. We may not need it all, but in this situation, I'd rather have it and not need it. I don't know what we'll be dealing with out there."

"What about the fishing poles?" Dave asked. "Should we throw them in?"

"Yeah, good idea. I didn't think about that, but you're right. They might come in real handy if we need to fish for food before this is all over with."

While Dave scurried to get the blankets and food, Sam found his cell phone and tried calling Jenny's father's cell phone. Nothing. No static, no busy signal. He stuck the phone in his pocket and gathered up everything he thought they might need to survive for a few days. He was thankful that he hadn't traded off his Dodge Mega-Cab 4x4 truck for a regular cab pickup, like he had considered doing the previous year. Right now, the extra room was going to come in handy. The camper shell on the back would protect everything they could stash in the bed.

After loading the truck, Sam went inside and helped

Linda to her feet. With his hand under her chin, he lifted her face.

Her normally sparkling blue eyes looked dull and listless.

Putting his hands on her shoulders, he gently shook her. "Linda. . . . Linda, can you hear me? Damn, Linda, I need you here with me right now. I'm not sure I can do this on my own."

When she didn't respond, he took her by the arm, guiding her out of the house. "Dave, why don't you sit in the back seat so you can keep an eye on your mom."

"Is she going to be all right?"

"I think so. She's in shock. She needs time to adjust to what's happening."

"Okay. What about Ashley?" Dave asked, concern for his sister evident in his voice. "Are we going to swing by Jenny's house and pick her up now?"

Sam started the truck. "Yeah, that's what I figured we'd do." *If she's alive.*

Chapter 2

Thirty-two-year-old Lisa Baldwin just finished eating dinner when the house started shaking. The cupboard doors opened, spilling pots and pans, cans of food, and boxes of cereal, all over the kitchen floor. She crawled under the table and watched in dismay as the doors on the china hutch came open and her grandmother's china slid out, shattering into millions of pieces on the tile floor. She curled up in the fetal position, protecting her face and head with her arms.

Lying there, she wondered what could have caused such a massive earthquake here in Wyoming. Her husband Shawn had talked a lot about the Yellowstone volcano before he had died. He was convinced it would erupt sometime in his lifetime. She used to kid him about having an obsession with it. He even went so far as to put together a Yellowstone emergency pack: a duffle bag full of survival gear. Now, thinking back on everything he'd said, she knew in her heart, this was the only thing that could have happened. Trying to keep her mind off of what was going on around her, and knowing that she would probably have to leave, she started making a mental list of what to take and what to leave behind.

When the earthquake stopped shaking the house, she crawled out from under the table. Enough light from the setting sun came through the windows to illuminate the room, even through the veil of dust, hanging in the air.

Lisa coughed. *I need to stop breathing in all this dust.* She looked around the kitchen. Finding a dish towel, she tied it around the lower half of her face and made her way through the mess into the living room. Coughing again, she realized the dish towel wasn't keeping the dust out. Returning to the kitchen, she poured a bottle of water on it, then retied it on her face.

She got the battery-powered radio out of the hall closet and listened for information, while throwing a few things together, just in case she really did have to leave. She knew she would have to travel light, which meant leaving behind almost all of her personal belongings and keepsakes. She took two pictures: one of her mom and dad, and one of her wedding day with Shawn. She stuck the pictures, a coat, a jacket, and a pair of gloves in a backpack, along with Shawn's Berretta 9mm, two extra magazines, and a box of shells. She grabbed a duffle bag and stuffed it full of clothes and a few personal items.

Hearing the reports on the radio confirming the eruption, she confirmed her own decision to leave, moving with more haste. She wanted to get on the road, ahead of the mad rush of humanity she knew would be leaving town.

She threw the backpack, the duffle bag, and Shawn's Yellowstone survival pack in the passenger's seat of the old 79 Ford F-250 4x4 Shawn had owned since he was in high school. Reaching behind the seat, she pulled out a sawed-off double-barreled shotgun that Shawn had kept in a special pouch, sewn on the back of the seat. It had a pistol-grip stock, and the barrels had been cut down to twelve inches, so that the overall length was less than sixteen inches. On their first date, when she'd asked Shawn why he carried the gun, he had told her it was for varmints, and not just the four-legged kind either.

She opened the glove compartment and removed a box of 12- gauge shells, setting them on the front seat next to the shotgun.

As she drove down the driveway, she glanced in her

rearview mirror, taking one last look at the house, not knowing if she would ever return. A tear ran down her face as a flood of memories flashed through her mind.

Ten years earlier, just after they had married, Lisa and Shawn looked at the 200-acre ranch, which had been for sale. They fell in love with the place and made an offer on the spot. The elderly widow eagerly accepted their offer and, almost before they knew it, the young couple owned a cattle ranch ten miles north of Gillette, Wyoming.

The first eight years had been good; the ranch was making money. Lisa and Shawn were living their dream-life. The only thing missing were kids. Although they both wanted kids, they had decided to wait until they were in their mid-thirties. The last two years, however, had not been so good. Her parents, who lived in Gillette, had died within a year of each other. Then, six months ago, Shawn had been thrown from his horse and broke his neck. He died a week later.

After Shawn's death, Lisa had hired Clem two days a week, four or five hours a day, to help her with the heavier work around the ranch.

"After what Clem tried to do to me today," she said, thinking back on what had happened earlier that morning, "I hope I never see his sorry, drunken ass again." As she drove away from the ranch, the incident with Clem ran through her mind.

* * *

She had gone into town to run some errands. As she pulled into the graveled yard next to Clem's old black 1964 Cadillac, she noticed the gate she'd asked him to fix stood wide open, and her two milk cows were headed for the highway and freedom. "Son-of-a-bitch. . . . Clem!"

she called out as she got out of the truck. "Clem, where are you?" She stormed into the barn. Hearing snores coming from one of the empty horse stalls, she looked inside.

Clem, head thrown back and mouth wide open, lay on his back on a pile of hay with an empty bottle of Jack Daniels next to him.

Lisa turned and picked up an empty water bucket. At the faucet by the watering trough, she filled it up. Back at the stall, she threw the water on Clem's face and stepped back as he rolled onto his side, coughing and sputtering.

"Aw, what the hell's goin' on? Why'd you go an' do that?"

"I'll tell you why. Because you're drunk. I'm not paying you to drink. I'm paying you to help me with the work around here." She set the bucket on the ground. "Although, I don't know why I pay you. You don't do hardly anything, and what you do manage to get done is usually so screwed up, I have to go back and redo it."

"Now, that's not true that I don't do nuthin' 'round here." He sat up and brushed hay off his shirt. "Why, jus' this mornin', I fixed that section of fence on the north side of the hay field."

She knew he was an alcoholic, but she had never seen him drink while he was working. Apparently, today he had decided to spend some time with his best friend Jack. "What about the loose gate to the corral? Did you fix that like I told you to?"

"Yupper, you bet. Fixed it up good as new."

"Good as new. Really. Then, how come the cows are out," she said, pointing toward the front yard with her voice raising, "and walking down the damned road?"

He stammered, "Well, I . . . umm . . . thought I fixed it. I'm sure . . . "

"I don't want to hear any more excuses. You're fired.

Get your stuff and get out of my sight."

"What 'bout my pay? I have money comin' to me."

Unlike most women, Lisa carried a wallet in her back pocket, which was a lot easier than carrying a purse everywhere she went. She pulled out some money and threw it on the hay. "Here's two-hundred dollars, that's more than I owe you. Consider the difference your severance pay." She watched his eyes as he glanced at the money, then back to her.

His eyes moved slowly down her body, then back up again. "That ain't enough," he said, slowly getting to his feet. "I want more."

"That's crazy. I'm not giving you one cent more."

"Money ain't what I want," he said as he lunged towards her.

She dodged to the side and stuck her foot out, tripping him.

He fell on his stomach and groaned.

As he rolled over, Lisa grabbed the pitchfork leaning against the stall and pointed the tines at him. "I'm not screwing around. Get ou . . . "

Moving fast, he whipped his foot up and knocked the pitchfork out of her hands.

She froze in fear as she realized he wasn't as drunk as he had let on. He had been putting on an act, trying to get her close enough to grab. Her heart skipped a beat. She swallowed hard as he stood up, looking a lot bigger than she had remembered. Her five-foot-six, one-hundred-thirty-pound frame could be easily overpowered by the two inches in height and fifty pounds he had on her.

"Now I'm gonna make you pay." He threw a round-house punch.

She ducked, but not fast enough.

His fist grazed the side of her head with enough force to stagger her. He grabbed her shoulders, trying to force her down to the ground.

Lisa screamed and kicked out with her cowboy boot, connecting with his right shin.

He let out a howl of rage, grabbed his leg, and balanced on his left foot.

She kicked his left shin, eliciting another roar of pain from him and causing him to fall. Turning, she ran from the barn, fearing the pain she had inflicted on him wouldn't keep him down for long.

"You bitch," he called after her. "I'm gonna kill you now. I'm gonna kill you nice and slow."

She ran to the truck and threw the door open. Flipping the seat forward, she grabbed the shotgun from its pouch. Pulling it out, she turned just as Clem staggered to a stop ten feet away. "Get off my land," she screamed, pointing the gun at him. "Now!"

He glanced from her eyes to the gun and back, then took a hesitant step forward.

She pointed the gun at his legs and pulled back one of the hammers. "I swear to God, I'll shoot you in the leg if you don't leave right now."

"No need to get upset, sweetheart. Put the gun down and let's talk about this. I'm sure we can settle our differences without you shooting me." He took another step towards her.

She moved the barrel of the shotgun slightly to the right and pulled the trigger.

Clem grabbed his thigh and fell on the ground. "Ya shot me! I can't believe ya shot me. Call an ambulance. I need to get to the hospital."

For a second, she wondered if she really did shoot him. *I'm sure I moved the gun far enough away. If anything, maybe one or two pellets might have hit him.* "Let me see your leg," she said, keeping the gun pointed at him.

He moved his hands.

She could see blood on his pants, but not very much. "You don't need an ambulance. You might have been hit by a couple of stray pellets, but you'll live. Now," she said with as much bravado as she could muster, "get up and get out of here."

She stood her ground until Clem's Cadillac turned onto the main highway and headed towards town. She herded the cows back into the corral and, as she shut the gate, she realized Clem had fixed it. He had just forgotten to shut it.

* * *

Now, driving down the highway, feeling sad and alone, her head filled with thoughts. *I wonder how long it will take before the ash is gone and I will be able to return? I wonder if I will even want to come back? There are so many memories there, good and bad.*

She sighed and thought about Clem. *Damn, that was too close. I never want to do that again. I thought I would really have to shoot him. Well, I guess I did shoot him . . . kind of. I wonder if he'll report me to the sheriff. If he does, it'll be his word against mine. Everybody knows he's a drunk and a troublemaker.*

She took a deep breath. *Well, it's over now. There's no sense in worrying about it. I'll never see him again. . . . I hope.*

Chapter 3

Sam drove to Breezy Acres, where Jenny's parents lived. The subdivision had been developed three years earlier by Sam's land-development company. Only a quarter of a mile from Sam's house, it was close enough for the two fourteen-year-old girls to walk to each other's homes.

As Sam drove through the neighborhood, the destruction caused by the quake looked eerily like something a tornado had blasted through the area. In the dim light of the setting sun, he could see that all the homes were heavily damaged. Many had completely collapsed, with debris strewn across the carefully tended yards and into the streets. Surprised to see so few people about, all wandering around in a daze, he assumed that many had not made it out of their homes.

As he got closer to Jenny's street, his uneasiness grew. He gripped the steering wheel so tight, his knuckles turned white. *She's going to be okay,* he told himself as he approached the intersection. He turned the corner and Jenny's house came into sight. His heart sank. The house was completely demolished, a big pile of broken wood and twisted metal.

He pulled into the driveway. "Dave," he said, "stay in the truck with your mom." Sam put on his coat, grabbed a flashlight, and walked towards the house while looking for signs of life. He climbed the pile of debris and called out Ashley's name, not really expecting an answer.

He shined the light around and found a small opening where the roof had not completely collapsed. Shining the light into the hole, the passage seemed to go down at least ten feet or more. For just a fraction of a second, he debated about going down. On one hand, the chances of finding anybody alive seemed exceptionally low. If he went down and was killed, what would happen to Linda and Dave? But, on the other hand, if he didn't go down and look, he would probably have nightmares about Ashley being alive and hurt, crying out for him, calling out for him not to leave her behind. Deep down, he knew there was only one choice.

He slowly entered the hole and had only gone about six feet when a small aftershock shook the remains of the house. The whole mass groaned and shifted. He looked up at the mangled roof, hanging over his head, and hoped it wouldn't collapse and trap him. When the aftershock subsided, he let out a sigh of relief and continued moving down. To his surprise, the hole had enlarged.

About four feet down, Sam saw an arm . . . a young girl's arm. In disbelief, he scrambled downward. He gently picked up the arm with his work-roughened hands and checked for a pulse. Nothing. Setting the hand down, he noticed a bracelet on the wrist. He'd seen it before. About six months ago, Linda had taken Ashley on a mother-daughter trip to Cheyenne. As a special treat, Linda had bought them matching bracelets.

As Sam held the small hand in his, tears ran down his face. He couldn't even begin to accept the fact that his little girl was gone. *This can't be happening,* he thought as he squeezed the small, delicate hand.

As he was about to let go, it squeezed back.

What the hell? Is she really still alive or am I just imagining things? He squeezed again and felt another squeeze. Ecstatic, he let go and slowly started moving debris. After clearing the upper half of her body, he looked at her face and was surprised to see her eyes open.

"Ash, are you okay?" He brushed the blond hair out of her eyes and saw her look of confusion.

"I think so. What happened, Daddy?"

"I'm not sure, but I think it was an earthquake."

"An earthquake?"

"Yeah, but we need talk about this later. Right now, we need to see if we can get you out of here. Can you move your legs, or are they trapped?"

She shifted her legs and looked up at him. "They aren't trapped. I can move them fine."

"Do you hurt anywhere, like your neck or your back?"

"No, I don't think so. Well, maybe my head. I think I hit it on something."

"When you hit your head, did you lose consciousness?"

"Yeah, I just started coming around when you found me."

"As long as your neck doesn't hurt, you should be fine. Okay, I'm going to try to lift you out. If you feel any pain or if your legs get stuck, tell me, okay?"

"Okay, Daddy."

Sam reached in, took her under her arms, and lifted. He was surprised that she slid out easily. Standing her next to him, he looked her over to confirm that she didn't have any injuries, just a few scratches and a bump on her head. He wondered if Jenny could have been as lucky. "Ash, where were you and Jenn when the quake hit?"

"I was in Jenn's room and . . . she'd just gone downstairs to get some drinks and munchies."

"What about her parents and her brothers? Were they home?"

"I think they were all in the living room watching T.V."

He sighed, knowing there was no way Jenn or her family could still be alive under the rubble. The only thing that had saved Ashley was the fact that she had stayed on the upper level, where a pocket had formed around her.

"Do you think they're still alive, Daddy?"

"I'm sorry, Ash. I don't think they could have survived."

She wrapped her arms around herself and shivered. "Couldn't we try something, anything, just to make sure?"

Noticing she was only wearing jeans and a t-shirt, he took off his coat and put it over her shoulders. "I guess we could, but there isn't a lot we can do. There's no way we can dig through all this debris."

"Can we at least call out her name and see if anybody answers?"

Although he felt it would be useless and take up valuable time, he thought maybe they should spend a few minutes calling out, just in case.

They slowly made their way through and over broken boards and twisted metal. Calling out Jenny's name, stopping, and listening for a response every few feet, they moved safely away from the house.

"I'm sorry, Ash, but I don't think any of them made it."

She stifled a sob, trying not to cry.

Sam knew he was running out of time. If he wanted to get out of town before the ash cloud hit, he needed to get going. He put his arm around Ashley and gently lead her away from the house. When they got to the truck, Sam said, "Dave, I want you to ride up front with me. Ash, why don't you ride in the back seat with your mom? That way, if she needs anything, you will be able to help her."

Ashley's eyes opened wide with fear when she saw her mother.

Linda sat staring straight ahead, mumbling to herself.

Her blond hair stuck up in a mess of knots. She was covered from head to toe with dust, grime, and pieces of food.

"What's wrong with her?" Ashley cried. "Is she hurt? Is she going to be okay?"

"She's going to be fine. She's just in shock. A little rest and she'll be good as new."

Ashley climbed in and slid next to Linda. "Don't worry Mom, I'm here now. I'll take care of you." She smoothed down Linda's hair.

Sam took a last look around the neighborhood. At the moment, he didn't see anyone. He jumped in the driver's seat and, as he started the truck, Dave said, "So what now, Dad? Where are we going?"

"South. We need to go at least four hundred miles to get clear of the ash cloud. I figure somewhere in central Colorado should be far enough." *I just hope we don't have any problems along the way.*

Chapter 4

Lisa needed to stop in Casper to fill up with gas and buy food for later. With the dark streets, she assumed the power was out in a large section of Casper and the surrounding area. "I hope I can find a station that still has power," she said out loud, looking out the window for a sign of lights. "If not, I may have to siphon gas out of somebody's car."

The drive hadn't been bad. She'd begun to see patches of snow along the roads. Traffic had been minimal. She assumed most people either didn't know what had happened, or were putting off leaving until it was confirmed. She'd heard conflicting reports on the radio. Two stations reported the incident as just an isolated earthquake and told people to stay in their homes. The other stations reported that the volcano did erupt, causing the earthquake. Half the experts on the radio told people to stay where they were, while the other half told people to leave. *No wonder nobody's leaving town; nobody knows what the hell's going on. I'm glad I left when I did. As soon as all these people start leaving, the roads will be a bitch to travel on.*

Lights ahead on the highway got her attention. When she drew closer, she saw a small gas station/convenience store and pulled in, remotely wondering why the power was still on in this part of town and nowhere else.

After swiping her credit card and filling her tank, she went to the women's bathroom, located on the side of the building. Washing her hands, she looked in the mirror. *God, what a mess I am.* Dust clung to her face and disheveled dark-brown hair. Bending over, she shook as much dust out of her hair as possible. Using her fingers, she combed through it, trying to make it look presentable. She washed her face, glad she never wore much makeup. She brushed the dust off her clothes.

Heading into the store, she gathered up all the canned food, potato chips, and beef jerky she could carry.

"Are you having a party or something?" the young man behind the counter asked as he rang up the food and put it in plastic bags.

"Haven't you heard what happened?" she said, a little shocked.

"Oh, you mean the volcano thing? Yeah, I heard about it, but my dad has a friend who works for the park service. He told my dad there's nothing to worry about. He said we're far enough south, we won't be affected."

"I'm not taking any chances. I'm getting as far from here as possible." After paying the clerk, she picked up her bags and walked out.

She piled the food on the passenger's seat and, as she pulled out of the parking lot, an older black Cadillac pulled in. It looked suspiciously like Clem's car. She couldn't see who was driving, but she got an uneasy feeling that it was him. A flash of fear welled up inside her. *Did he follow me?* Her hands started to shake as she looked in the mirror. *No, why would he? It's just my imagination playing tricks on me. I'm still upset about the whole incident, that's all. I'm sure there are lots of cars around that look like that.*

As she pulled onto the road, she took a quick look over her shoulder. Before a sign blocked her view, she caught a glimpse of a man in a cowboy hat walking into the store. He was limping.

Chapter 5

As Sam drove down Interstate 25, heading south towards Casper at 110 miles-per-hour, he only heard the sound of the wind, whistling past the windows, and the tires, howling on the highway. Everybody else was fast asleep: Dave in the passenger seat, Linda and Ashley in the back seat. *That's good. They need it. It's been a rough day for all of us.*

As he drove in the dark, only the headlights of the truck revealing the road, he turned the radio on low and learned that the government was now telling everyone within six hundred miles of the Yellowstone area to leave immediately. It surprised him that there wasn't all that much traffic, considering the amount of people that should be evacuating the area. He figured he had left before most of them, and he wanted to keep going as fast as he could to stay ahead of the mad rush.

His thoughts turned to his older brother, Jerry, who lived in Medford, Oregon. Sam hoped Medford was far enough west that it wasn't affected by the volcano and ash cloud. Sam made a mental note to call Jerry the next day and make sure everything was okay. *Hell, we might even go stay with him and Sandy for a while, at least until we decide whether or not we can go back home.*

Sam was thankful it was a clear night and not snowing. He was sure the government was glad, too. They were going to have their hands full, evacuating millions of people away from the moving ash cloud. He could only imagine the problems they would face trying to evacuate huge numbers in the middle of a good-old

Wyoming blizzard.

When he arrived at the outskirts of Casper, the traffic started getting heavier, so he decided to skip the main part of town and make his way around it on the back roads. He felt pretty good about his decision until he saw a traffic jam ahead of him. Now, he wasn't so sure.

"Wake up, everybody," he called out as he surveyed the scene through the windshield. Cars sat in the road, jammed up against each other. People ran everywhere. It looked like a riot.

"What's happening?" asked Dave, rubbing the sleep out of his eyes.

"Yeah, Dad?" said Ashley, sitting up and looking around.

"I'm not sure, but I think all these people are trying to get out of town. It looks like a real mess. I'm not sure I want to try to get through that." Sam watched three different fist-fights break out and heard gunshots coming from deep in the jumble of cars.

A man drove up behind Sam's truck and blared his horn as he swerved around him. The man's brakes locked up, causing the car to slide into the side of a minivan. The man jumped out of the car with a gun in each hand. He ran into the mess of vehicles, firing at everyone.

From the back seat, Linda said, "Sam, I don't like this. I'm scared something bad is going to happen. Let's get out of here."

It flashed through Sam's mind that Linda sounded better. *Good, the shock must be wearing off.*

He glanced to his left and saw a medium-sized man walking up to the truck. It only took a glimpse for Sam to see that the man was not all there. He looked insane. Climbing up on the running board, he yelled something in a language Sam couldn't understand.

Sam watched in disbelief as the man stepped back,

pulled out a gun, and pointed it at the window. Sam threw the truck into reverse and floored it. "Everybody, get down," Sam yelled as he swerved, trying to avoid the bullets flying around the truck. A small hole appeared at the bottom of the windshield as a bullet punched through, spraying Sam with tiny shards of glass. He crouched lower, hoping none of the bullets would hit anything critical.

Once he was far enough away, sure they were safe, he stopped. He sat immobile, trying to calm his nerves. His hands shook so bad, he kept them gripped on the steering wheel. As he stared out the windshield at the chaos of people and vehicles in front of him, he heard a moan from the back seat. A sense of foreboding hit him as he quickly glanced around.

Ashley, with a look of horror on her face, gaped at her mom, while Linda stared down at the blood slowly staining her shirt bright crimson red.

"Oh, no, no, no," he cried as he looked with dread at the bullet hole in her shirt. Now, he could see that the bullet had passed through the windshield, gone through the seat, and hit Linda right in the middle of her chest. She needed help badly.

He sat forward, threw the truck into drive, and floored it. The big V-8 roared, leaving twin black snakes on the pavement as he headed towards the hospital he'd passed earlier. "Ashley," he called out over his shoulder.

"Yeah?" she replied, her voice trembling.

He tried to remember the basic first-aid he had learned years earlier. "Okay, Ashley, I need you to help me here. Grab a towel or a shirt, anything you can find, and put it on the wound and apply pressure."

"Okay."

He turned on the dome light so she could see what she was doing. In the rearview mirror, he watched her fumble around for something to put over the wound.

"Here, Ashley, use this," said Dave, handing her the dish towel he had used at the house to cover his mouth.

She took it and gently set it against Linda's chest.

"Ash, honey, you need to put pressure on it to help stop the bleeding, okay? Can you do that for me?"

Intently watching her in the mirror, the blare of a horn suddenly snapped his attention back to his driving. He realized he had missed a stop sign and a pair of headlights were coming at him from the right side of the intersection. He jerked the wheel to the left and slammed on the brakes. The truck slid sideways, bashing the tires into the curb, slamming Sam's head against the driver's window. The left side of the truck tilted upward. He feared it would roll over, but luckily, it righted itself and came to rest on all four tires.

Sam shook his head and blinked his eyes to clear his vision. "Ash, are you and your mom okay back there?"

"Yeah, I think so."

"Okay, good. Make sure you keep pressure on that towel."

"We're good, Dad," said Dave. "Let's go."

Still determined to get Linda to a hospital as soon as possible, Sam took his foot off the brake and pushed down the gas pedal. As the truck started forward, it pulled to the right. Sam turned the wheel to the left as far as it would go. The truck still went to the right. He shut the ignition off, got out, and walked around to the passenger's side. One look told him the truck wasn't going anywhere. Instead of the tire hitting the curb, which was an unusually tall curb, the right rear rim had hit it, bending the rim. "Shit," he muttered to himself.

The car he had almost hit, a late-model Jeep Liberty, sat by the curb. *If I explain the situation, maybe the driver will understand and help me get Linda to a hospital.*

The Jeep's door opened and a huge African-American man got out.

Sam's eyes widened in disbelief. He figured the guy was easily six-foot-eight-inches and weighed in at 280 to 300 pounds. His head was completely shaved, except for a small goatee on his chin. Even under the dim lights of the street lamps, Sam could see the muscles rippling underneath his tight t-shirt. "I'm dead meat," Sam said quietly as the man walked towards him. "I . . . um . . ." Sam stammered.

The man held his hands up with his palms facing Sam. "It's okay, Mister, I'm not going to hurt you. I'm a doctor. I just wanted to make sure everybody's okay. You hit that curb pretty hard."

"Did you say you're a doctor?"

"Yes, I am."

"Oh, thank God. Linda, my wife, she's been shot and needs help."

"Where is she?"

"Come with me. She's in the truck. I was trying to get her to the hospital. That's why I ran that stop sign."

"Let me grab my coat and my medical bag."

As the doctor went to get his bag, Sam heard him talking to someone and saw a woman get out of the car.

The doctor said, "By the way, I'm Richard Adams, and you are?"

"Sam . . . Sam Jones."

"Sam, this is my wife, Jean. She's an R.N. She's going to help me with your wife."

"Okay, that's fine," Sam said, glancing at her.

She stood about five-foot-six and weighed around 160 pounds. She wore light-colored scrubs, contrasting with her black short hair and chocolate skin. Sam estimated the couple to be in their fifty's.

At the truck, Richard opened the door, took one look at Linda, and said with authority, "We need to move her out of the back seat and put her over there on the sidewalk, under that light. Do you have any blankets we can lay under her?"

"Yeah," Sam said, "I have a four sleeping bags and a couple of blankets in a big box in the back of the truck. I'll get them for you."

Dave opened his door. "I'll help you get them, Dad."

Sam and Dave prepared the blankets. With the help of Richard and Jean, they gently moved Linda out of the truck and onto the blankets.

"Sam," Richard said, "why don't you wait in the truck with your kids?"

"My kids will be fine. I want to be with Linda, in case she needs me."

Taking Sam by the arm, Richard gently guided him back to the truck. "I can understand why you want to be with your wife right now, but think about your kids for a minute. Don't you think they're a little bit concerned about their mother, too?"

Sam studied Richard. He glanced at Linda, lying on the blankets. He looked at Dave, standing by the truck with his arm around Ashley. "I don't know . . . " Sam started to say.

"Dammit, Sam," Richard growled, "I don't have time to stand here while you think about what to do. Now, go over there and console your kids, while I do what I can for your wife."

Sam sighed. It wasn't like Richard was giving him a choice in the matter. "All right, but if she needs me, yell, and I'll be right there." Sam turned and called to the kids, "Get in the truck where it's warm." He climbed into his seat and started the ignition. He flipped the heater on high.

"Do you think Mom's going to be okay?" Dave asked.

"I honestly don't know, Son." When nothing more was said, Sam turned on the radio. "Maybe, while were waiting, we should see if we can get the latest updates on the volcano and ash cloud." He couldn't believe how many radio stations were playing music, instead of giving the people the news and information they needed for survival. He finally found what he wanted.

"The National Weather Service is reporting that the ash cloud is now as far north as the Canadian border. To the east, it's forty miles west of Buffalo. To the south, it appears to be sixty miles north of Casper, and to the west it has . . . "

Sam flipped back to one of the stations playing country music. He didn't need to know how far west the cloud had traveled. The only direction he cared about was south, and the cloud was getting too close for comfort.

After about thirty minutes, he heard a knock on the back of the truck. It was Richard. "Wait for me," he told the kids. "I'll be right back."

Richard's face looked tired and somber.

Anxiously, Sam asked, "Well, how's she doing?"

He shook his head. "I'm sorry, Sam. I did everything I could, but the damage was too severe. I couldn't save her."

Sam felt like someone had just reached inside his chest and ripped out his heart. He stood there confused, numb, not sure what to do.

Richard put his hand on Sam's shoulder. "Why don't you go over and sit with her for a few minutes? We'll keep an eye on the kids for you."

Sam shuffled to Linda's side and knelt next to her body, covered with a blanket. He gently pulled the blanket off her face. She looked so peaceful, like when she was sleeping.

He thought about their life together. This wasn't how he thought it would end. No one else knew that he and Linda had filed for divorce just the previous week. They had met in California the year he had graduated from high school. He had stayed with his grandma for the summer in L.A., where he had met Linda on the beach. By the end of summer, they had fallen in love and were married that fall. But after twenty years of marriage, they both had changed, had drifted apart, like a lot of couples who got married at an early age.

Six months ago, when he had found out she was seeing someone else, he hadn't been surprised. He'd noticed that, in the last few years, they hadn't been connecting. He'd thought about seeing someone, too, but he was so busy at work, he didn't have the time or energy to put into another relationship.

Despite their emotional separation and drifting apart, they had been happy for many years. *I wouldn't have changed anything*, he whispered to her, *even if it were possible. You gave me two great kids and you were a good wife. Thank you.*

After a few silent moments, he carefully covered her face and stood up. Now came the hard part: telling the kids. He wasn't sure how to go about it.

He slowly walked towards the truck, trying to figure out what to say and how to say it. *Just to tell them outright.* He figured that would be the best way to handle it now.

He opened the truck door. "Dave, Ashley, please come out for a minute."

As Dave climbed out, he asked with concern in his voice, "How's Mom doing? Is she going to be okay?"

Sam tried to control his emotions as he looked at them. Tears welled up in his eyes. "Dave, Ashley, I'm so sorry. She didn't make it. The doctor did everything he could for her, but the damage was too much."

Ashley ran into his arms and sobbed.

Dave came right behind her.

Sam didn't know how long they stood there, holding each other as they cried. All he could think about was the fact that Linda was dead and, somehow, he felt like he had let her down by not protecting her.

Richard stepped next to Sam. "I know this is a bad time for all of you, but I really need to talk to you for a minute."

"Dave," Sam said, "why don't you and Ashley get back in the truck and wait for me? It's getting cold out here and I don't want either one of you to get sick."

Dave wiped his eyes and helped his sister into the truck.

As Sam followed Richard, he said, "I want to thank you for trying to save Linda. I'm sure you did everything you could, under the circumstances."

"I'm sorry I couldn't do more. Even if we could have gotten her to the hospital's trauma center, they couldn't have saved her. The damage was far too extensive." Richard stopped about thirty feet from the truck. "Why don't we talk here?"

"Yeah, sure." Sam saw Jean walking towards them. "Hi. Thank you for your help with . . . " Sam nodded in the general direction of Linda's body, looking out of place on the sidewalk.

"You're welcome. Are your children doing okay?"

"They're fine, for now. I don't think it's hit them yet."

"So, what are you going to do now?" Richard asked, looking at Sam.

"I guess I need to take her to the morgue or something, don't I?"

Richard sighed. "I'll make this short and sweet: you have a hard decision to make about what to do with

Linda's body."

"What do you mean?"

"You haven't forgotten about the ash cloud that's headed towards us, have you?"

It took a second for Sam to register what Richard was talking about. "Oh, shit, I was so concerned about Linda, I forgot all about it."

In a quiet, hard tone, Richard said, "Well you had better start thinking about it, because in about two hours, everyone in this town will be dead."

"What you're trying to tell me is that we need to get out of here ASAP, and that I don't have time to take Linda anywhere? Is that right?"

"That's right. So, like I said, you have a decision to make. Are you going to stay here with your wife, who is already beyond help, or are you going to take your kids and get the hell out of here while you still can?"

"But I can't just leave her here, can I? I mean, shouldn't I at least take her to the hospital or something."

In a much softer voice, Richard said, "Listen, we work at the hospital. We just came from there. You don't want to go anywhere near that place right now. It's a total madhouse. Even if you took her there, there's no way you could convince anybody to look at her. I don't want to be an asshole, but she's dead, Sam. There's nothing anybody can do for her."

"He's right," Jean added. "As hard as it seems, it's the right thing to do for the kids' sakes."

"Okay, I see what you're saying, but I don't know. It's just too hard to conceive just leaving her here without letting someone know she's here. I mean, what's going to happen to her?"

"The same thing that's going to happen to all these other people when the ash cloud gets here. It's going to bury them under about two feet of ash . . . dead or alive . . . forever."

"They're right, Dad."

Sam spun around, momentarily speechless as he saw Dave and Ashley standing to the side. "How long have you been standing here? What did you hear?" His eyes flashed with anger as he studied them.

"We've been here long enough to know what you have to do," Ashley said as she wiped her eyes.

Dave took a step forward. "Dad, I know it's going to be tough, but there's no sense in all of us dying, just trying to do what we think is morally right. You know Mom would freak out if she thought you were considering putting us in danger by staying around here."

Debating what he should do, Sam looked at his kids. "I guess you're right. Are you sure you're okay with this?"

"Yes," they both said in unison.

"Okay, so I guess . . . "

"Sam," said Richard, "can I make a suggestion? Why don't you take the kids and go for a short walk. Let me and Jean take care of her body."

"Are you sure?"

"Yeah, I'm sure. Don't worry about it. We'll take care of everything."

"Okay . . . thanks. I owe you one."

Sam and the kids walked up the street and sat down on the curb in front of the truck. In a companionable silence, they watched the traffic pass by. Sam hadn't noticed before, but the traffic seemed to be getting heavier with more people trying to get out of town.

He started thinking about the fight he and Linda had right after the quake. He realized that, along with sorrow and grief, he was also feeling a large dose of guilt. *I shouldn't have been so hard on her. She was just worried about the kids.*

"Are you doing okay?" Dave asked, interrupting Sam's thoughts.

"What? Oh, yeah, I'm doing as well as can be expected under the circumstances. How about you?"

"This sucks, big time," he quietly said as he wiped his eyes.

Sam, sitting between them, put his arms around both and pulled them against his chest. "Go ahead and cry," he said. "It's okay to mourn for your mom."

After fifteen minutes, Richard called out. "We're done."

Sam got up and dried his eyes. On the way back to the truck, he said, "Dave, will you pull the spare tire out and start replacing the bent rim on the truck while I talk to Richard for a minute?"

Dave nodded and got started, while Jean motioned for Ashley to come over to her car.

Sam asked, "So, Richard, what's the best way to get out of town?"

"I know a roundabout way that will get us out with a minimum amount of traffic." With raised brows, Richard inquired, "It is okay if we travel with you, isn't it?"

Sam was a little stunned. "You want to travel with us?"

"Sure, why not? Were all headed south, so we might as well travel together. That way, we can help each other out if we need to."

"Yeah, sure, that sounds great." Sam felt a sense of relief, knowing he wouldn't have to deal with everything by himself.

* * *

A little later, as Sam followed Richard's taillights out of town, he was surprised that, even though he saw lots of traffic, it was moving along pretty smoothly. He'd always thought, in a situation like this, everybody would behave irrationally, creating complete chaos. *Of course, it was chaos in places, like in Casper, where I lost Linda. . . . No, I can't think about her right now. I need to concentrate on the kids. I'll have time later to think about her, when I'm alone.*

Chapter 6

Sam looked at his watch: 7:15 a.m. They had traveled about eight hours. The traffic grew heavier the further south they drove. The kids had finally fallen asleep in the back seat. Now, on Highway 13, just over the Colorado state line, he had only been able to go about thirty-miles-an-hour most of the time. Sam had to keep reminding himself to stay calm. At least, they were moving, slowly, but they were moving. The sun just cleared the ridge to the east, glaring off the snow-covered hills. It looked like it was going to be a nice day, not a cloud in the sky, as far as he could see.

He'd been listening, periodically, to the radio for updates on the ash cloud. The latest information reported it had traveled as far east as Buffalo and as far south as Rawlins, Wyoming. Now, it was moving at about forty-miles-an-hour. *Let's see, how far is it to Rawlins from here? It can't be more than about a hundred miles. With the traffic moving so slowly, we're barely staying ahead of the ash cloud.*

In other news, the first woman President of the United States, Veronica Hamilton, had declared the eruption of the volcano and the ensuing ash cloud a national emergency. In all areas of the country that were expected to be affected by the ash cloud, she declared Martial Law, which meant the military was now in control. And since Veronica was Commander in Chief of the military, that meant she was in complete control of the country. She had moved out of the White House, since it was in the path of the ash cloud, to Beale Air Force Base in central

California. She ordered all military bases not in the direct path of the ash cloud, to send all non-essential personnel east and south along the projected path, to help with evacuating the millions of people fleeing the cloud.

Not a fan of Veronica's, it bothered Sam that she would leave those military bases with only a skeleton crew to protect them. He reached over and shut off the radio, which was probably a mistake, since he started commiserating about Linda and the fact that, by now, her body was buried under the ash. He forced himself to stop thinking about her. *It isn't time yet.*

He flipped his sun visor over the side window. Looking at his gas gage, he saw he was down to a quarter of a tank. He grew concerned about running out of gas, but every station he had passed was packed with people. He'd even seen fights break out in the lines as he drove by. Luckily, he always kept his tank full. He remembered when he had gotten his first car. He was always running out of gas.

One day, his dad told him, "It costs the same to run on the top half as it does to run on the bottom half, so you might as well keep your tank full. "

Since then, he had become almost fanatical about having a full tank of gas.

On Highway 13, almost to Craig, Colorado, Richard turned off the main highway onto a small two-lane road with snow banks on both sides. Sam wondered where in the hell he was going, but figured Richard knew his way, and that was good enough for Sam.

After about four miles, they rounded a snow-covered hill. Sam saw a small gas station and convenience store, straight out of the 1950's. A service bay and small office sat on one end, with the store on the other end. The snow had been plowed out of the parking lot and stocked in piles over ten-feet tall. *They must get a lot of snow here,* he thought.

Richard pulled into the station and stopped at the antique-looking gas pump.

Sam pulled up on the other side of the pump, closer to the building. "Dave, Ashley," he called over his shoulder. "Time to wake up."

Dave sat up, rubbed his eyes, and looked out the window. "Where are we?"

"Just outside of Craig, Colorado."

"Good, it's about time we stopped," said Ashley, sitting up and pushing the hair out of her face. "I have to go to the bathroom real bad."

Sam got out and walked around the truck to the pump, where he ran into Richard, who was stretching out his giant six-foot-eight-inch frame.

"I've been through here before." Richard said. "I remembered this place and figured it was far enough off the main road that they might still have some gas left."

"After all the confusion we saw at the other stations, I'm glad you knew about this place. I'll go see if I can find somebody to help us with these pumps. They're so old, I don't know how to work them."

As Sam rounded the corner of the truck, the attendant, dressed in greasy coveralls, came out of the service bay. He wiped the grease off his hands with a rag greasier than his hands. His hat was so dirty, the words on it couldn't be read. His nametag identified him as *Bubba*. He called out, "Yawl need some gas?"

Sam held out his credit card. "Yeah, fill both vehicles."

"Sorry, cash only, and it's twenty dollars a gallon."

Sam stopped dead in his tracks. "Twenty dollars a gallon? You're kidding me, right? Your sign says four-twenty-four a gallon."

Bubba put his hands in his pockets and smiled,

showing a mouth full of rotten teeth. "Nope, I heard all the stations down on the highway are sold out. There's a big demand, ya know, so I decided, based on the law of supply-and-demand, I would raise my prices and make a little extra money."

Before Sam could tell Bubba what he thought of him, Richard stepped around the back of the truck, grabbed Bubba by the front of his greasy coveralls, and shoved him up against the side of the truck. Bubba's head bounced off the camper shell, his grease-covered hat knocked to the ground.

Sam smiled at the dark stain appearing in the area of Bubba's crotch.

In a low, menacing voice, Richard growled, "You miserable little prick. I ought to beat the living shit out of you for trying to take advantage of us. But today is your lucky day. I don't have time to mess with you right now. So . . . this is how it's going to work. You're going to fill our tanks, then you're going to charge it to that card." Richard nodded his head toward Sam. "And you had better make damn sure that you only charge us your advertised price. You got that?"

"Yes," the man murmured under his breath.

" Yes, what?" Richard yelled, shaking him.

"Yes, Sir," Bubba blurted loudly. "Right away, Sir."

Richard let go. He chuckled as he watched Bubba scurry away. "I hated to do that, but sometimes, you gotta do what you gotta do."

"I may not know you very well," Sam, said with a chuckle, "but I can tell that you enjoyed scaring the hell out of him, didn't you?"

"Yeah, I guess I did enjoy it a little bit. Sometimes being a big black man has its advantages."

While Bubba filled the gas tanks, Jean, Dave, and Ashley went into the diner to use the bathroom and freshen up.

After Sam told Richard what he had heard on the radio, Richard said, "Well, at least we're staying ahead of the ash cloud. If the traffic stays as light as it has been, we should be okay." He pulled out a map of Colorado and spread it out on the hood of his Jeep. "I think our best bet is to stay on Highway 13 until we get to Interstate 70 here at Rifle." He pointed to a spot on the map. "By my estimate, that should be a good four hundred miles from Yellowstone. The radio station Jean and I listened to interviewed a scientist from some volcano research institute. He estimated the ash cloud will only go about that far south. Once we get to I-70, we can find a road heading south and look for someplace to settle in and rest until we figure out what we're going to do." He handed Sam a business card. "This is my cell phone number. I checked my phone and I have service, so as long as your phone works, you should be able to call me if you need anything while we're on the road."

"That's a good idea." He took the card and exchanged it for one of his own from his wallet. "Here's my number. I guess I'd better check my phone and make sure it works." He went to the truck and got his phone. After making sure he had service, he said, "Okay, were good to go as far as communication goes. I'm going to run in and take a leak. Do you mind staying out here and keeping an eye on Bubba?"

"No, go ahead. I'm fine."

Sam passed Jean and the kids as they came out of the store with white plastic bags. He looked from the bags to Jean. "What did you do, buy out the whole store?" he jokingly asked.

"No, not the whole store. But I did get all of us a hot meal. I hope you like fried chicken and burritos. That's all they had already hot. This place also sells a few groceries, so I bought a bunch of non-perishable food for later."

"Thanks," Sam said, "that was good thinking, getting the extra food. Even if I didn't like chicken and burritos, I'm so hungry, I'd eat them anyway." He let the screen door slam behind him as he entered the store.

Chapter 7

Eight hours after Lisa had left Casper, she was driving down Highway 13, almost to Craig, Colorado. Traffic grew heavier the further south she drove. She needed gas, but all the stations she had passed were out.

Up ahead, in the early morning light, she saw a small two-lane road, branching off the main highway. Over the last few miles, she had wasted precious time and fuel by taking two other roads, just like this one, in failed attempts to find gas. She couldn't say exactly why, but suddenly she knew, she was supposed to take this road. *What the hell,* she thought as she turned off. *I've got a fifty-fifty chance, either way I go.*

She looked in the rearview mirror for the black Cadillac she was sure had been following her. She wasn't certain, but she thought she'd seen it twice since leaving Casper.

Now, as she rounded a bend in the road, she saw a black car turn onto the same road. "Damn. I'm almost positive that's Clem. I've seen that car too many times now. That can't be just a coincidence." *Well,* she thought, *I dealt with him once before. I guess I can deal with him again.* Her eyes glanced at the shotgun laying on the seat.

The black car passed her.

She looked to see if it was Clem, but she only caught a glimpse of the driver, flipping her the bird through the open window.

He swerved in front of her too soon, clipping her front bumper.

"Oh, shit," she cried, her truck careening off the road,

right into a small clump of trees and a snow bank. The impact sent a shower of icy snow billowing into the air.

She unbuckled her seatbelt and climbed out, mentally checking herself for injuries. Satisfied she wasn't hurt, she pulled on her coat and turned her attention to the truck. It hadn't fared so well. A cloud of steam rose from under the hood. A tree branch had gone through the grill and punctured the radiator. Taking off her cowboy hat, she slapped it angrily against the hood, then shoved it back on her head. She yelled at the retreating car. "Screw you, you son of a bitch!"

Knowing she couldn't stay out in the cold, she hurried to the passenger's side and started gathering her stuff. *Maybe I can hitch a ride to the nearest town and try to find another car.*

Only a mile from the gas station, heading back to the main road, Sam noticed an older pickup truck sitting about thirty feet off the road and partially buried in a clump of small trees and a snow bank. As he got closer, he saw a figure in a bulky coat and a cowboy hat standing next to it.

Richard's brake lights came on as he pulled off the road and stopped.

"Shit," Sam said, "what's he doing? We don't have time to be good Samaritans and help this guy out." He stopped the truck, threw open his door, jumped out, and stomped over to Richard's SUV. As Richard opened his door, Sam complained, "We don't have time for this, you know."

Richard took off his sunglasses and glared at Sam. "Yes, we do."

Sam threw his arms in the air. "Okay, fine." He followed Richard towards the truck.

About fifty feet away, the cowboy turned and said, "That's close enough."

They both stopped in their tracks.

Sam realized it wasn't a man. It was a woman, a good-looking woman. She held a sawed-off shotgun against her hip and pointed it straight at them. *Oh, God, not another crazy with a gun.* He looked around for something to hide behind if she started shooting.

Richard put his hands up. "Hey, it's okay, lady. I'm a doctor. I just stopped to see if anybody was hurt."

She warily looked him up and down. "You're a doctor? You don't look like one. You look more like an NFL linebacker."

"Yeah, I know, I get that a lot, but I really am a doctor. I'm Richard Adams, and this is my friend Sam Jones." He nodded towards Sam. "We're traveling together."

"Where are you coming from?" she asked guardedly. "And where are you going?"

"We came from Wyoming," Sam answered. "We're going south, trying to stay ahead of the ash cloud that's coming this way."

She glanced at their vehicles, then lowered the gun.

Sam took a quick glance over his shoulder. Jean, Dave, and Ashley had gotten out of the vehicles and were standing by the truck. He assumed that seeing a woman and two teenagers had helped convince her they weren't going to hurt her.

"Yeah, well, I was, too, until that crazy asshole ran me off the road in his mad dash for gas. Now, my truck's wrecked, and I'm stranded here, unless . . . " She let her words trail off as she looked at them, hope showing on her face.

"Well," Sam said, "if you want to, I guess you can come with us." He shrugged his shoulders and looked at Richard like, *What the hell are we supposed to do, leave her here?*

"I was hoping you'd offer," she said as she turned and

started pulling things out of the truck. "By the way, I'm Lisa."

Richard elbowed Sam in the ribs and whispered, "I thought we didn't have time for this."

Sam shot a look at him and saw a shit-eating grin on his face. Sam smiled. "We don't. But since we're here, we might as well help her out. It'll give Jean somebody to talk to besides you." He hoped Richard would take the hint and let Lisa ride with him.

"All right, I'm ready," she said. "Here, take this." She shoved a duffle bag into Sam's hands and headed for his truck.

"Now, that's a woman that doesn't mess around," said Richard.

"No shit," Sam murmured as he hurried to catch up with her. Approaching the truck, he said, "Since we're in a hurry, I'll make the introductions quick. This is Lisa. Lisa, this is Richard's wife Jean, and my kids, Dave and Ashley. Now, if you don't mind, can we get the hell out of here before that ash cloud gets here and buries our asses?"

Lisa glared at him. "I'm just waiting for you to tell me where I'm riding, Mr. Impatient."

"She'll have to ride with you, Sam," Richard said, trying to hold back a laugh. "We don't have any room in the Jeep."

"That's fine with me," Sam shot back. "I don't care where she rides, as long as we get going." He gave her a fleeting look. "Throw your stuff into the bed of the truck and get in." He turned on his heel and stomped towards the truck, not sure if he was more angry at Richard for insisting that Lisa ride with Sam, or at Lisa for being so outspoken and, somehow, making him feel like a chastised schoolboy.

She opened the rear window of the camper shell,

threw in everything except for a backpack, slammed the window shut, then climbed into the passenger's seat. "Well, what are you waiting for? You were in such a hurry to get going. Floor this thing and let's get out of here."

He glared at her, shrugged his shoulders, and floored it, throwing dirt and gravel out the back as he roared onto the road. Glancing in his rearview mirror, he looked at the kids to see how they were handling the situation.

Ashley had her head tilted back on the headrest with her eyes closed, like she could care less.

I'm kind of worried about her, he thought. *She hasn't said much since Linda died.*

Dave, on the other hand, stared out his window with intense anger on his face.

Well, it looks like Lisa's already got one of the kids pissed off at her.

Sam reached over and turned on the radio to get an update. Already tuned to a station in Craig, the reporter announced that the ash cloud was approaching the Colorado state line, only thirty-eight miles away. "Shit," he quietly swore under his breath as he looked at his watch.

"Hey," Lisa snapped, "you didn't have to stop and help me. I would have figured something out."

He glanced at her. "I'm sure you would have. You probably would've car-jacked some poor family's car and left them stranded. . . . Well, it's too late to worry about it now. All we can do is hope the traffic keeps moving along, or we're going to be screwed."

If looks could have killed, he would have been dead from the glare she gave him. "You're such an asshole." She shook her head.

Covertly, he studied her as she removed her coat and hat. She wore a tight-fitting t-shirt. He couldn't help but notice how she filled it out sufficiently well. *Nice body, fit and trim.* It looked like she worked out a lot . . . not a lot of muscle, just firm and toned. He figured her to be in her early thirties. Her dark brown, almost black hair fell down about six inches below her shoulders.

The thing about her that totally captivated him, though, were her eyes: the most brilliant shade of baby-blue he had ever seen. When he looked into them as she had given him the *killer look,* her fiery passion had awakened something deep in his soul.

The corner of his mouth turned up with the slightest smile as he turned his attention to the road ahead. *She's a fascinating lady. I don't know why she affects me the way she does. On one hand, I want to strangle her, and yet, at the same time, I'm strongly attracted to her. I've got a feeling this is going to be an interesting trip.*

Chapter 8

Passing through Rifle, Colorado, without any major problems, Sam was pleased to see that the Highway Department had opened the east-bound lanes of I-70 to west-bound travel only. Still, the freeway couldn't handle the amount of vehicles heading out of harm's way, and traffic moved at only thirty- to thirty-five-miles-an-hour.

Sam called Jerry on his cell phone and they chatted a few minutes.

"I'm glad to hear the you and Sandy are doing okay," Sam said. "The kids and I are facing a lot of new challenges, but we're going to be fine."

"Why don't you bring your family to Medford?" Jerry offered. "We've got lots of space and would love to have you."

"I appreciate the offer. I'll think about it. A lot of people are probably heading over to the coast of Washington and Oregon, so I'll get the kids someplace safe south of here. Then, I'll think about heading up to Oregon."

"You'd like this town. It's quiet and friendly. Just know, the offer is always open."

* * *

After passing through the outskirts of Grand Junction, Richard pulled over on the shoulder of Highway 50, a two-lane road heading southeast.

Sam got out of the truck. He noticed Lisa getting out, also. As she pulled on her coat, he glanced from her to the truck. "Why don't you wait in the truck where it's warm?"

"Why?" she said sharply. "I have as much say in this as either of you, don't I?"

"Alright, whatever." As he turned, he muttered to himself, "Jeez, don't get your panties in a bunch."

She covered the ten feet between them surprisingly fast and shoved him so hard he stumbled to stay on his feet. "My panties are none of your business, asshole."

Astounded at the suddenness of her actions, Sam looked for support from Richard, who walked toward him with a smile and a shake of his head. Giving her a mock bow, Sam said, "Fine, whatever you say, sweetheart."

"I'm not your sweetheart." Without missing a beat, she turned to Richard. "Why did we stop here?"

Richard chuckled and pulled his coat collar up over his ears. "This road goes east for about ten or twelve miles, then turns south, towards Delta, and further south, Montrose. I figure that should be far enough to get us clear of the ash cloud. I just hope we can find a place to stop and rest that isn't overly crowded."

Her brow furrowed in concern, Lisa asked, "Do you think that's going to be a problem?"

"I honestly don't know. You've seen all the traffic on the freeway. Hell, look at all the traffic on this road." He pointed to the steady stream of cars, trucks, vans, motor homes, motorcycles, and even a few bicycles passing by. "They're all going in the same direction as we are. The question you have to ask is, where are they all going to end up?"

Sam broke in. "The way I see it, if all else fails, we can camp out."

Richard's jaw dropped. He looked at Sam like he was insane. "Are you nuts? It can't be more than forty-five degrees out here right now, and it's going to get a hell of a lot colder than that tonight. In case you didn't notice," he said, pointing to some hills about ten miles away, "that white stuff up there is snow. What do you propose we do, build an igloo and huddle together for warmth?"

Sam laughed. "No, when I left home, I threw in all of our camping gear. I've got a ten-by-fourteen cabin tent that's big enough for all of us to sleep in. Plus, I have sleeping bags and blankets, gas stoves and lanterns, pots, pans, and utensils. Hell, I even have a small generator and a TV-VCR combo-unit so we can watch movies if we want to."

Richard shook his head. "You're unbelievable, you know that? You really expect us to live in a tent, like some sort of gypsies or something?"

"No, hang on a minute," Lisa interjected. "He may be right. True, it might not be the best accommodations, but all these people are going to get crammed into refugee camps, churches, gymnasiums, anywhere someone can find to stick them. Do you really want to be cooped up in a room with all these people? I know I don't. I'd rather take my chances in the tent."

"Well, it's something to think about," Sam said as he glanced at the long lines of cars going by. "I think we need to get going. You and Jean can talk about it and let me know what you want to do the next time we stop."

"Okay, I'll think about it," Richard responded. "I think you're right. We do need to get going."

On the way back to the truck, Sam said to Lisa, "By the way, I'm sorry about that panty remar . . . "

She doubled up her fist and punched him on the shoulder. "Jesus, you're such an idiot." She stomped off and ripped open the truck door.

Sam stood there, not quite knowing what to think. He'd never met anyone quite like her. On one hand, she was self-confident and full of fire, and yet, on the other hand, she was impulsive, blunt, and unpredictable. *Maybe that's what bothers me,* he thought. *She's unpredictable. Despite that, I kind of like her. I just need to watch what I say from now on.*

* * *

Lisa climbed into the truck and slammed the door. She silently cursed Sam for being such an asshole.

Dave said quietly, "Everything okay?"

"Yeah, everything's great," she replied sarcastically. Grabbing hold of her anger, she softened her tone. "I'm sorry. I didn't mean to take my frustrations out on you."

"That's okay. We're all going through a tough time right now, what with the volcano erupting, dealing with the ash cloud, and us losing our mom and everything."

Turning around in surprise to look at him, she asked, "What do you mean, you lost your mom?"

"She was shot last night in Casper." He wiped his eyes with his coat sleeve. "Richard and Jean tried to save her, but . . . they couldn't." He turned away, obviously too choked up to continue.

Ashley, lying with a pillow over her head, stifled a sob. Her petite body shook uncontrollably in the throes of sorrow.

Blindsided by this sudden revelation, Lisa wondered if she should say something to comfort Ashley. Before she could speak, the truck door opened and Sam jumped in. *Good,* Lisa thought, *I'll let him handle this. Ashley's his kid. Besides, he'd probably get mad at me if I tried to console her.*

Sam started the truck and inched toward the flow of traffic. Keeping his eyes on a spot to merge into the line, he never once looked back to check on his kids.

Just like a man . . . clueless when it comes to emotions.

Lisa discreetly studied him out of the corner of her eye. He didn't act like a man who had just lost his wife a few hours before. Although curious about how his wife had ended up getting shot, she didn't think it would be too couth to outright ask him about it now. She decided to wait until he or someone else mentioned it. *What is it about him that brings out the bitch in me?* she wondered. *It seems like everything he says or does pisses me off. Maybe it's just that our personalities clash.*

After enduring a half-hour of silence, Lisa felt the urge to talk. Turning sideways on the seat and curling her legs up under her, she looked toward the back seat and observed the kids sleeping. In a soft voice, she said, "So, do you want to talk or not?"

His brown eyes glanced at her. "Sure, why not? I haven't got anything else to do."

She figured it would be safe to start with a little small-talk. "Okay, so where are you from?"

"Buffalo. How about you?"

"Gillette," she said with interest. "I guess we were almost neighbors, weren't we?"

"Yeah, I guess . . . if you consider someone living sixty miles away from you a neighbor. . . . Okay, now it's my turn to ask you a question." He seemed a little nervous, his fingers twitching on the steering wheel. "Why did you get so upset earlier? What was it about the panty comment that pissed you off so bad?"

"Oh, shit," she said, bouncing her head off the headrest. "Would you please just forget about it. It was nothing. I overreacted, that's all." Closing her eyes for a moment, she took a deep, calming breath. "Listen, I'm sorry if I seemed a little bitchy earlier, but the last eighteen hours have been a little bit stressful, don't you think?"

He sighed. "You're right. I probably shouldn't have

made that comment about your panties in the first place. It was insensitive and inappropriate. I'm sorry. Will you forgive me?" Before she could answer, he blurted, "Tell you what, how about if we start over? Hi, I'm Sam Jones, and you are?"

Yes, she would forgive him. Hell, she wasn't really mad at him, but she wanted to keep control over the situation so it didn't get out of hand, like with Clem. *I shouldn't answer too fast. Let him think I'm really upset.* She looked at him for a full minute, then finally said, "Okay, here's the deal. I'm willing to forgive you for the panty remark and start over if you will do one thing for me."

He gave her a serious look. "All right, and what would that be?"

"Will you please find a bathroom. I really have to pee."

He laughed. "No problem. In fact, I could use one myself. Do you want an actual bathroom or will a big bush do?"

"I'd prefer a real bathroom, but if you can't find one, a big bush will do. By the way," she said, sticking out her hand, "I'm Lisa Baldwin, and I'm pleased to meet you, Sam."

Chapter 9

With the heavy traffic on the road, lines moved at ten to fifteen miles-an-hour. After sleeping for a few hours while Dave drove, Sam felt refreshed. He now sat behind the wheel as they approached Montrose, Colorado, where the traffic had slowed to a crawl. "This reminds me of rush hour in L.A.," said to no one in particular as the truck crept forward another few feet.

Lisa responded, "It looks like the police are keeping everyone out of the parking lots, which are already full." She pointed at a cop yelling at a minivan trying to enter a parking lot.

Sam watched as the driver of the minivan leaned out his window and gestured wildly with his arms, then pointed to the parking lot, then to the cop. "They're probably directing everybody to the other end of town, filling in parking lots as they go."

"That poor man probably has family in there," Ashley said quietly. "They ought to let him in so they can be together."

Dave interjected, "If the cops try to match up families, this place would be more of a nightmare than it is."

A haggard-looking police officer finally directed Sam into a shopping-center parking lot. A strip of snow-free grass, about ten feet across, separated the parking lot from the road.

Sam parked against the curb and shut off the engine. Looking in the visor mirror, he ran his right hand through his dark-brown, naturally curly hair. His dark eyes, staring back at him, looked weary. Stretching his stiff neck muscles, he turned to face the passengers. "It looks like we'll be here for a while, but before you get out, I want to set some ground rules, so listen up. First, don't get out of sight of the truck. Second, use the buddy system. I want two of you together at all times. Third, keep your eyes and ears open. It looks calm enough right now, but with this many people around, it could turn ugly pretty quickly. If there's trouble, get in the truck, pronto. Any questions?"

"I have to go to the bathroom," Ashley said, squirming in her seat and looking out the window, "and I don't see one anywhere. Where am I supposed to go?"

"It has been awhile since our last restroom break," Sam said. "Give me five minutes and I'll set up the Porta Potty."

"A Porta Potty?" Lisa asked doubtfully. "You expect us to use a Porta Potty with all these people standing around watching us?"

Sam chuckled. "Relax. It has an enclosure around it. It's completely private."

Lisa, Dave, and Ashley climbed out of the truck. They stretched and loosened up their muscles, which, like Sam's, had probably begun to cramp from sitting for such a long time.

Sam reached into the glove compartment and took out a .40 caliber Glock Model 22. He stuck it in his pants at the small of his back. *Just in case,* he thought. As he exited the truck, he pulled on his coat.

Richard and Jean approached as Sam opened the tailgate of the truck. Richard said, "We're going to take a walk, loosen up our legs."

"That's a good idea," Sam replied.

"While we're out and about, I'll ask around to see if I can find someone in charge." Richard studied the masses of people swarming everywhere. "We need to know what they're going to do with all these people. I doubt this town has the resources to take care of this many refugees. We might have to go further south to find a place to stop."

"Can I go with them?" asked Dave.

Sam looked from Richard to Jean. "Do you mind?"

"No, not at all," said Richard. "It might be a good idea to have him with us. The more eyes and ears the better."

Sam hesitated, worried about letting Dave out of his sight.

"Don't worry, Sam," Jean said quietly. "We'll take good care of him."

"Okay, but be careful," Sam said as he pulled the Porta Potty out of the truck. "Remember what happened in Casper. These people may be desperate. You never know what they might do." As he bent over to set the Porta Potty in the middle of the grassy area, the back of his coat rode up.

"Yeah," Richard said, "I see you learned your lesson and you're prepared to defend yourself this time." He pointed to the pistol in the waistband of Sam's pants. "That's good, but you may want to keep it covered up. It may not be a good idea to let anybody know you have it." He turned, took Jean's hand, and the three of them walked off toward a group of official-looking people.

Ashley pressed her legs together, hopping from foot to foot. "Dad, could you please hurry? I have to go really bad."

"Okay, okay, give me two minutes. All I need to do is put up the privacy screens."

"Wow," Lisa remarked, "you really do have everything we'll need to camp out, don't you?" With her coat wrapped around her, she had stretched out on the dead brown winter grass.

"You bet," Sam said with a chuckle. "It's

funny . . . when I was younger, I could camp for a week with just a sleeping bag and what I could carry on my back. It seems like the older I got, the more stuff I needed. I figured, if I was going camping, I might as well be comfortable. When the volcano erupted and we had to decide what to take with us, I didn't know what conditions we would face, so I threw in all our camping stuff, just in case we couldn't find a place to stay. Now, I'm glad I did." He looked at Ashley and nodded toward the Porta Potty to let her know he was finished with the screens and she could use the make-shift bathroom. "I think I'll clean the truck up a little. After last night, it needs it." He opened the doors and started gathering up the garbage, folding the blankets and pillows, and rearranging the cab.

After Ashley finished her business, she helped him rearrange the camping gear in the bed of the truck.

When they were done, Sam asked Lisa, "Would you like a blanket to lie on?"

"No thanks, I've always loved lying on the grass, even grass like this." She pulled up a small clump of the dead winter grass. "I remember when I was a little girl, maybe five or six, my mom and I would go out in the backyard and lie down to watch the clouds as they drifted past. We saw all kinds of shapes: rabbits, bears, frogs. Once, we even saw an elephant, trunk and all. Mom called it our 'special time.' Nobody else could join us. Just the two of us. I would lay my head on her stomach, and she would run her fingers through my hair. God, I miss her." With her eyes closed, her face held a calm, serene look.

"How long ago did she die?" Sam asked, assuming her mother had died from the sound of her words. He enjoyed listening to her voice and wanted to keep her talking. He could picture the two of them: Lisa and her mother lying in the grass, watching the clouds.

"About eighteen months ago. My dad died ten months before that."

He sat down on the grass next to her. "I'm sorry, that must have been hard, losing both of them so close together."

"Thanks, it *was* hard."

"Do you have a husband or kids?"

She opened her eyes, the peaceful, serene look on her face dissolving into one of irritation. She jumped up and brushed the grass off her pants. "I think I need to take a walk, stretch my muscles a little bit." She turned and quickly walked away.

He stood up, feeling he had somehow offended her. "Wait a minute," he shouted, "did you forget about the rules? Remember, the buddy system: two people together at all times."

She stopped and slowly turned around with a hard look on her face. "Contrary to what you may believe, I can take care of myself." She pulled aside her coat and lifted the front of her shirt, displaying the butt of a handgun stuck in the waistband of her pants. "And yes, I know how to use it. And if I have to, I will."

Sam stepped forward. "I'm not doubting your ability to take care of yourself. I'm sure you're competent, but I'm going to have to insist. If you're going to travel with us, that makes you one of us, which means you'll have to follow the rules, just like everybody else."

"He's right, Lisa," Jean said firmly, apparently hearing the last part of the conversation as she, Richard, and Dave approached. "We're all in this together. If one of us won't follow the rules, that puts the rest of us in danger. There's no room for that kind of behavior here. You either follow the rules or you leave."

Sam hadn't heard Jean speak so many words since he'd met her. He was shocked at the bluntness of her statement.

"That's right," added Richard. "After you hear what we just learned, you'll understand why it's so important that we all stick together."

Lisa bowed her head and closed her eyes for a second, as though she was trying to let go of her anger. When she opened them again, she made eye contact with Sam. "You're right, I'm sorry," she said humbly.

"Apology accepted." Sam kept eye contact with her until she looked away. Turning to Richard, he said, "Okay, what did you find out? It sounds bad."

"It is. Basically, the governor of Colorado declared a state of emergency, then he declared martial law, and from what I heard, the way they are handling it isn't pretty."

"Who are *they*?" Ashley asked, walking from behind the truck. "And what are they doing?"

Richard replied, "*They* are the Military, the National Guard troops, and the local police. They're going around gathering everyone's weapons: all firearms, hunting bows, cross bows, and hunting knives with a blade longer than two inches. Basically, anything that could be used as a weapon. They've also imposed a curfew. No one is allowed away from their sleeping area from dusk until dawn. The penalty, if you are caught, is being thrown into the local jail, which, from what I hear, is standing room only at the moment."

"Can they do that?" Dave asked. "This is America. Don't we have the right to keep our guns?"

"Under martial law," Richard explained, "they can do anything they want. That's the problem. It gives the Military complete control. It removes all power from the executive, legislative, and judicial branches of the government. And that's not the worst of it. They're forcing everyone to 'donate' *all* their food to the food bank. In return, we'll each be allowed one meal a day. I saw the meal, and it wasn't much. One piece of bread, one big scoop of beans, and a scoop of rice. That's it."

Lisa asked, "That's not very much. Can a person even survive on that?"

"Barely," Richard answered. "You'd waste away to skin and bones, but you could survive."

Sam asked, "What happens if I don't give up my weapons and food?"

Before Richard answered, a man yelled, "No, I won't!"

About twenty yards away, stood a group of five solders, M-16's slung over their shoulders, semi-auto handguns in holsters on their hips, and batons in their hands. They formed a half-circle around their leader, a stocky man facing a man and a woman. The couple, both dressed in jeans and flannel shirts, stood in front of an older mini motor home.

"This is bullshit," the man yelled. "There's no way I'm giving you my guns or my food. I've seen that slop you're feeding people, and I've talked to people who've already given their food to you, canned foods like soups, chili, tuna fish, spaghetti, corn, and beans. Why aren't you feeding people that? Or are you keeping all the good stuff for yourselves?"

"That's none of your concern," said the apparent leader of the solders. "Are you going to give us your weapons and food, or are we going to have to take them?"

"I'm not giving you shit," the man said defiantly, taking a step back toward the motor home.

The leader swung his baton, hitting the man on the upper arm.

Even from twenty yards away Sam, heard the sharp crack of the bone breaking. He was horrified.

"Son of a bitch," the man yelled, grabbing his arm and falling to his knees in pain. "You broke my damned arm."

The solder laughed. "Tough shit, you shouldn't have refused to give us your weapons and food. Now, you don't have a choice. We're taking them. And since the jail's full, you're getting kicked out of town." He nodded his head at the other soldiers, who quickly moved forward, picked up the man, and handcuffed both the man and his wife.

Lisa stared at Sam. "Well, I guess that answers your question, doesn't it?"

"Well, this sucks," Sam said, watching the couple in the handcuffs. "I don't want to give the soldiers anything, but I really don't want a broken arm either."

"There are a couple of options available to us," Richard ventured. "Options that we may want to consider."

Everyone turned to him. "The first option, which I'm not crazy about, by the way, is leaving town and finding somewhere to camp, as Sam had mentioned earlier. The second option is to continue heading further south, into New Mexico or Arizona, maybe even California."

"What about Oregon?" Sam asked. "My older brother Jerry and his wife live in Medford. He's already asked me to come stay with them for as long as we want. I'm sure he wouldn't mind if I brought a few friends along."

Richard grimaced. "Oregon's a long way from here. Do you think we could make it with the roads being such a mess?"

"I don't know." Sam shrugged. "It might be worth trying."

Jean offered, "I'm thinking Arizona would be good. The weather will be better, and the further south we go, the more normal things will be."

Sam studied her. "Do you have relatives or friends in

Arizona that would take us in?"

"No I don't, but I'm sure we could find someone that would be willing to help us."

"Wait," Lisa said eagerly, "I know a guy that lives in Arizona. He went to high school with Shawn, my husband. He lives in the desert near a town called Lake . . . Lake something. Let's see, I'm trying to remember."

"Havasu?" said Sam. He was surprised by the reference to her husband. *I'm going to have to ask her about that later.*

"Yeah, that's it. Lake Havasu."

"Lake Havasu?" asked Richard. "I've never heard of it. Where's it at?"

Sam explained, "I watched a documentary about it on the Discovery Channel a couple of years ago. It's on the Colorado River, about two hundred miles south of Las Vegas. If I remember right, in 1960-something, a guy named McCullough started a town by the lake. He bought the London Bridge from England, had it shipped overseas, and reassembled it in the desert town. I think there's around fifty thousand people living there now."

Jean spoke up. "I vote we leave. Like Lisa said, the further south we go, the more normal things should get."

"I agree," said Richard. "I'll follow you when we leave town."

"Dave, Ashley, what do you think?" asked Sam.

"Someplace warm sounds good to me," Ashley responded as she stood shivering in her coat.

"Count me in, too," Dave quickly added.

"Okay, that's good," said Sam. "We're all in agreement. Let's get out of here before those goons come over and try to take our stuff. Dave and I will take down the Porta Potty and screen while the rest of you get ready to go. Ashley, why don't you keep watch? If you see any solders heading this way, let me know, okay?"

She nodded and walked to the parking-lot side of the truck to get a better view.

* * *

A short time later, as Sam headed the truck toward the exit of the parking lot with Richard's vehicle behind him, he noticed Lisa staring intently out the window. "Is there something out there I should know about?" he asked with concern.

"No, I thought I saw a familiar car is all."

"It wouldn't surprise me if you did. I'm sure we're not the only ones from back home that drove down here."

She replied with a nod of her head, then started chewing on a fingernail.

I wonder if there is something about the car I should know about?

Before he could ask, she pointed out the window. "Oh, oh. I don't think they want us to leave."

The same disheveled cop that had directed them into the parking lot waved his arms at them to halt.

Sam rolled down his window and stopped the truck, leaving it in drive.

"And just where in the hell do you think you're going?" snarled the cop, peering into the cab.

This guy's got an attitude, just like the soldier that broke the man's arm. Shit, I hope this doesn't get violent. Sam wasn't a good liar. His heart skipped a beat as he considered what to say. In the most confident voice he could muster, he said, "We talked to the people in charge here about how all these refugees are taxing the limits of your resources. They agreed it would be better for you and your town if we continued heading south until we got to an area that hasn't been overrun quite so badly."

"I assume the car behind you is leaving also?" the cop asked, looking back at Richard's Jeep.

"Yeah, we're traveling together," Lisa offered, leaning forward in her seat.

"Did you donate your food to the food bank?" the cop asked.

"Yes, we did, but they let us keep just enough to get to the next town." *Did I answer too quickly? he wondered.*

The cops eyes narrowed. He looked at Sam suspiciously. "Now, why don't I believe you?" He moved his right hand to the butt of his gun and took a step back.

Oh, shit, now what? He looked out the windshield at the line of cars turning into the parking lot. He suddenly noticed that a car had stalled, creating a gap in the line. The cop who had been standing in the road directing traffic walked to the distressed owner of the car. Just beyond them, heading south toward freedom, sat the empty road. With the uneasy sensation of a swarm of butterflies being set loose in his stomach, he nervously contemplated the consequences of what he was about to do. *God, I hope this works. I don't want anybody else to get killed.* He flashed back to Casper and the night Linda was shot.

Sam smiled at the cop standing next to the truck, then floored the gas pedal. As the truck lurched forward, he earned a short scream of surprise from Lisa, who flew back in her seat. He shot through the gap in the traffic. Checking his rearview mirror, he saw Richard tailing right behind him.

The cop, rather than pulling out his gun and shooting them, threw his arms up in the air in a gesture of defeat, then walked away shaking his head.

Sam sighed in relief.

"Nice move," said Lisa, nodding her head in appreciation.

"Thanks. Sorry I couldn't give you any warning, but I didn't want the cop to know what I was going to do. Hell, I didn't even know what I was going to do until I did it." He broke into a nervous laugh. "Are you two okay back there?" he asked the kids over his shoulder.

"Yeah, I'm fine," Ashley said quietly.

"That was *awesome*, Dad," Dave said animatedly, slapping the back of Sam's seat.

Sam looked at Ashley in the mirror.

She smiled. Other than looking a little pale, she seemed fine.

When Sam checked Dave's appearance, he was shocked to see Dave grinning from ear to ear.

Dave's flushed face and wide-open eyes shined with excitement. He looked wild, like he was on a ride at Disneyland, or like he was high on drugs.

As Sam studied his son's face in the mirror, grim thoughts ran through his mind. *It looks like he's getting used to all this danger. Actually, he's enjoying it. I've seen that same look on the faces of adrenaline junkies, and I'll be damned if I'll let him turn himself into one of those. I'll have to keep an eye on him. If it looks like this is going to be a problem, I'll have to have a little talk with him and straighten him out. Great, just what I need: one more thing to worry about.* He took a long, deep breath and slowly let it out, then turned his attention to the road ahead.

* * *

To help him stay awake as they headed toward New Mexico, Sam listened to the radio off and on, getting updates on the volcano and the ash cloud. The latest information wasn't good. The cloud had fanned out from the epicenter and now covered most of the states in an easterly and southeastern direction. The initial blast had sent ash as far south as Salt Lake City. From there, the jet stream had carried it to Denver and on to Charleston, South Carolina. The states from eastern Wyoming to Maine reported varying amounts of ash, from two feet or more in Wyoming to just a dusting in Maine.

In keeping with President Hamilton's declaration of martial law, all military bases in the unaffected areas had retained only security people at the offices. All other military personnel were being sent east and south to evacuate, care for, and control the flood of refugees streaming out of the path of the ash cloud.

Sam couldn't say exactly why, but the thought of leaving all those military bases with only a skeleton crew bothered him.

Traffic seemed fairly light after they had left Montrose. It took only four hours to get to Farmington, New Mexico. Sam was surprised at how easily they obtained gas, food, and a motel for the night. Jean had been right: the further south they went, the more normal everything seemed to be.

I hope everything stays normal, he thought. *I can't believe what we've been through in the last twenty-four hours. I'm not sure what we're going to find in Arizona, but it's got to be better than where we've been.*

Chapter 10

The next day, traveling west on Interstate 40, roughly an hour from Lake Havasu, Arizona, Lisa said, "Sam, can I talk to you a minute?"

From the tone of her voice, he sensed she had something serious on her mind. "Yeah, sure." He glanced toward the back seat to make sure the kids were still asleep.

Lisa looked out the window as she said, "Remember yesterday, when we were leaving Montrose, and I thought I saw a familiar car?"

"Yeah, what about it?" He started getting an uneasy feeling in his stomach.

"I think it's behind us."

Sam looked in his rearview mirror and saw two cars. "Which one? The silver one or the black one?"

"The older black Caddy."

"I have a feeling I'm not going to like the answer to this," he said grimly. "Is someone following you?"

"I think so, but I'm not sure." She nervously ran her fingers through her hair. "I swear I've seen that same car four times now since I left home."

"Why would it be following you?"

"Because," she replied hesitantly, "if it's who I think it is, I kind of . . . um . . . shot him."

Sam slowly turned his head and stared at her. "You *kind* of shot him? How do you *kind* of shoot somebody?" *Oh, great, what have I gotten myself and the kids into now.*

"I shot next to him . . . with a shotgun. One or two

pellets hit him in the leg."

Sam glanced down at the butt of the shotgun sitting next to her leg.

"Don't worry," she said, "I'm not going to shoot you."

I wonder if that's what she told the last guy she shot. He let out a long sigh. "I think you'd better start at the beginning and tell me the whole story."

Dividing his attention between the Caddy and Lisa as she told him the story of how she had shot Clem, Sam watched her transform from a self-confident, bold woman to a scared little girl. This shocked him. When she finished, he said, "Do you really believe he would follow you clear down here?"

"I don't know. It's possible isn't it?" she quietly asked.

"Well, if it's him, we're about to find out." In the mirror, Sam watched the Caddy pull up along the side of the truck. A chill went up his spine. He swallowed hard. "Is that him?" he asked, pressing back into the seat to give her a better view.

The self-confident woman suddenly returned as she leaned forward and studied the man driving the passing car. "No, it isn't." She gave a sigh of frustration, then slumped back in her seat.

"You sound disappointed," Sam said, watching the Caddy return to the right-hand lane further up the road.

"I guess, in a way, I am. I'm tired of looking over my shoulder all the time and wondering if or when he'll show up."

"Hell, there must be thousands of old Caddy's like that still on the road. The reason you never noticed them before is because you weren't looking for them, not until this thing happened with Clem. Chances are, he didn't even make it out of Gillette before the ash cloud hit. If he did, I don't think he would be crazy enough to follow you a thousand miles just to get even for putting a couple of shotgun pellets in his leg."

"You're probably right." As she stared straight ahead, she bit her lip. "But, what if he *did* follow me?"

Annoyed with her irrational worry, Sam blurted, "Look, you can spend the rest of your life looking over your shoulder if you want, but I think you'd be better off just forgetting about it. Anyway, it sounds to me like he's the kind of guy that wouldn't dare try anything if there were other people around, so, for the next little while, just make sure you're never alone."

"Yeah, you're right," she conceded. "I need to just forget about him. Like you said, he probably didn't make it out before the ash cloud hit." She turned her head and looked out the side window.

Sensing that the subject was closed, Sam turned his attention to the desert scenery. The vegetation in this area of Arizona consisted mostly of Palo Verde trees, Mesquite and Ironwood bushes, and three or four different kinds of cacti, including one that looked to Sam like a teddy bear. Large, perfectly flat sections of desert, covered with black rocks, looked like parking lots. *This place makes Casper look like a tropical paradise,* he thought, mentally comparing the sun-baked, near-colorless desert to the lush green vegetation of his home state. *I wonder if I'll ever go back to Wyoming ... to home? I think I'd rather live in Oregon with Jerry than live in a god-forsaken place like this.*

He glanced at Lisa. Her eyes were closed, her head rested against the side window. From the rearview mirror, he saw the kids sound asleep. *It doesn't matter where I end up. As long as the kids are happy and I'm happy, we'll be okay.*

* * *

A little while later, as they approached the exit for Lake Havasu, Lisa broke the silence. "We should stop and look in a phone book for John's phone number and address."

Sam looked at her in disbelief. "Are you telling me you don't know how to contact this guy?"

"Of course I know how to contact him. We look in a phone book, find his number, and call him."

"What if his number's unlisted, or what if there's more than one John . . . ? What's his last name again?"

"Red Feather."

"Red Feather? Is this guy an Indian or something?"

"No," she said, rolling her eyes, "he's Native American."

"Whatever. So, what makes you think you'll be able to find him?"

"I don't know. Maybe I can't, but we'll never know unless I try."

"I guess not," Sam said, pulling onto the off-ramp and heading toward a Pilot Truck Stop.

While the rest of his companions went inside to use the bathroom and get drinks, Sam filled the gas tanks.

Lisa stood at the pay phone booth and searched through the *White Pages*.

When she returned to the truck, Sam asked, "Well, did you get hold of him?"

"As a matter of fact, I *didn't*," she replied sharply. "I called his house and no one answered, so I wrote down his address from the phone book and asked the guy working inside how to get there. He said we already passed it. We need to go back the way we came, about three miles to the first exit east of here: Franconia Road. From there, we just follow the map the clerk kindly drew for me." She waved a piece of paper in the air. "We shouldn't have too much trouble finding his house."

* * *

Leaving the gas station, Sam headed east to the Franconia Road exit. For eight miles, he bounced over the network of unpaved roads that crisscrossed the desert floor. Some roads crossed the plentiful dry washes, while others followed the path of the washes, forcing Sam to put the truck into four-wheel drive so he wouldn't get stuck in the sandy bottoms. *I'd hate to be caught in one of these washes in a thunderstorm,* he thought as he crossed a particularly wide wash.

"Look, there it is," shouted Lisa excitedly. "That's the fence post the man told me to watch for. I'll bet that's John's house."

Looking up the hill, Sam saw a tan-colored mobile home with dark-brown trim and a corrugated skirt covering the base. It nestled against the foothills of a small mountain range a half-mile away. The address on the fencepost matched Lisa's handwritten note, so Sam turned off the main dirt path and headed up the two-track road.

The land developer in Sam surfaced as he got closer. "Man, talk about living in the middle of nowhere. They didn't even plow the vegetation out of the way. They just pulled that mobile home onto a semi-bare spot and parked it." He stopped in front of the house. "There's no real driveway, unless you count the two ruts leading in here as one. At least, power comes in, and they're probably on a well for water and a septic tank for sewer."

"John never was a flashy person," Lisa responded. "He told me once that he would rather spend his money on things he wanted, rather than spend it trying to keep up with the Jones's."

"Well, it's nice to see he believes in having some basic amenities, like satellite T.V." Sam pointed at the satellite dish on the roof.

Parked in front of the house sat a late-Eighty's Jeep Cherokee, painted in desert-camouflaged colors. An added four-inch lift and oversized tires modified the vehicle for desert travel. A winch, a handyman jack, and a shovel had been mounted on the front bumper. A spare tire and two five-gallon gas cans had been attached to the back door. All four doors and the back hatch stood open, exposing boxes and bags inside. A blue tarp, covering the roof rack, hid a bundle of goods overhead.

"It looks like your friend is going somewhere," Sam remarked.

"Yeah, you're right, it does look that way doesn't it?" Lisa opened the door and climbed out of the truck.

"Who are you and what do you want?" a man yelled from inside the house.

"John, is that you?" Lisa called out as she stepped forward. "It's Lisa Baldwin, Shawn's wife."

The man, wearing blue jeans and a white t-shirt with the word "WHAT?" in large black letters across the front, walked out the front door and stopped at the top of the steps. He looked to be in his late thirty's, about five-foot-seven, weighing around 150 pounds. He wore his jet-black hair in a short, military crew-cut.

"Lisa," he cried as he hurried down the two rickety wooden stairs, "I'm so glad you got out of that mess up north alive. I've been thinking about you from the moment I heard about the volcano erupting." He crossed the hard-packed dirt of the yard. Grabbing her in a bear hug, he swung her around in a circle. Then, he held her at arm's length. "You haven't changed a bit since the last time I saw you. What's it been, three years?"

"Actually, it's been four. You look the same, too, other than your great tan. You must be out in the sun a lot these days."

"Yeah, I am. I've been doing a little prospecting here and there."

Sam cleared his throat as he approached them. "Hi, we aren't interrupting anything here, are we?" He motioned toward the Jeep.

"No, not at all. We just got back from doing a little grocery shopping in town."

Lisa put her hands on her hips and lifted one brow. "Wait a minute . . . who is this 'we' you're referring to? Is there something you need to tell me?"

He chuckled. "Her name is Jennifer Davenport, but she likes to be called Sunshine. She's inside. When we go in, I'll introduce you."

"Okay." Pointing at all the shopping bags inside the Jeep, she said, "Now, what's with all these groceries. It looks like you bought out the whole store."

"We only go into town once a month, so we stock up on everything we'll need for the month." He looked over her shoulder at the kids and Richard and Jean as they approached. "So, tell me, who are all these people you brought with you?"

"Well, this is Sam, and his kids, Dave and Ashley. This is Richard and Jean. We've been traveling together since we met in Craig, Colorado."

"Hi, it's nice to meet all of you." He looked at Lisa. "Are you going to stay for a few days?"

"We were hoping we could. Do you mind?"

"Of course not. You know I would do anything for you." He gave her another hug.

Sam looked more closely at the mobile home, probably built in the 1960's. The joints where the siding came together had begun separating. The skirting around the base, hiding the axles and tires, looked ready to fall off. *I don't want to stay here. This place is a dump. It looks like John picked it out of some junkyard. Worse yet, it's probably full of spiders and scorpions.* Not wanting to offend John, Sam said offhandedly, "The rest of us can get a room in the closest town. We don't want to inconvenience you."

"Nonsense," said John with a wave of his hand. "You're more than welcome to stay here. However, we have only one extra bedroom, so some of you may have to sleep on air mattresses on the floor."

"What do you think, Jean, Richard?" Lisa asked. "Do you want to stay here or not?"

Jean gave Richard a barely perceptible nod of her head.

"I will stay here on two conditions," Richard stated bluntly. "First condition: Jean and I get the bedroom."

"That's fine with me," Lisa offered quickly. "I don't mind sleeping on the floor. You should have the bedroom anyway, since you're the only married couple in this group. Isn't that right, Sam?"

"That's right," he replied amiably. *Shit, how am I going to get out of this without hurting anybody's feelings?* "The kids and I are used to sleeping on air mattresses when we go camping. It won't bother us a bit."

"Okay, second condition. We'll agree to stay here if you'll let us help you haul all this food inside." Richard smiled at John.

"Hell, I can't argue with that." John held out his hand. "Richard, it's a real pleasure to meet you. Grab a handful of bags and come on in."

They all grabbed sacks and boxes of food and followed John into the house.

As Sam entered, the interior shocked him. While the outside was shabby and in disrepair, the interior was neat and clean. A leather couch, a love seat, and two reclining chairs had been evenly spaced around the living room.

Two knick-knack-covered tables stood in the corners. A coffee table, sitting on a large woven Navaho rug, occupied center-stage in the middle of the room. The pictures on the walls depicted desert scenes, tying into the overall southwestern theme. Soft music, with flutes and tom-toms, resonated from the stereo. *Hmmm, I guess it might not be that bad staying here, after all.*

"Wow," Lisa whispered to Sam, "I didn't expect it to be so nice in here."

"Yeah, quite the contrast between the outside and the inside, isn't it?" He followed her through the living room and into the kitchen.

"Set the bags on the table or on the counter tops," John said. He turned and yelled into another room, "Honey, we have company."

A voluptuous blond, wearing Levi 501 cut-offs and a skimpy pink halter top, walked into the room.

Damn, there's nothing like tight buns in 501's, Sam thought, looking her over discretely. *This just keeps getting better and better. I think I might change my mind about staying here.*

John said eagerly, "Lisa, I would like you to meet Sunshine. Sunshine, this is my friend Lisa."

Lisa held out her hand. "Hello, it's nice to meet you."

"Hi," Sunshine's emerald-green eyes sparkled as she shook Lisa's hand. "I'm so glad to meet you. John has told me a lot about you."

After Lisa introduced the whole party to Sunshine, Sam assisted the others in hauling the rest of the food into the kitchen and helped them put it away.

John prepared drinks for everyone, then led them out the back sliding door to a covered redwood deck. Once they were settled on the patio furniture, which consisted of six padded chairs and a free-standing swing, Sam, Richard, and Lisa gave John and Sunshine a brief overview of their trip, leaving out the worst parts.

As they told their story, Sam could see the concern and worry on Sunshine's face. She kept looking at John as if they were passing silent messages back and forth.

When they were done, Sunshine announced, "You're all going to stay here as long as you need to." She held up her hand as if she knew they would protest. "And don't worry. It's no imposition. It will be nice to have people around for a change."

Richard responded with a friendly smile. "We really appreciate the offer. It's been a hard, stressful trip, to say the least."

Finally okay with the situation, Sam said, "I would love to stay here for a few days."

"Good," said Sunshine. "It's settled then."

Ashley leaned over and whispered something to Dave.

He nodded, then looked at Sam. "Dad, is it okay if Ash and I go for a walk? We've been sitting a long time and need to stretch our legs."

"Yeah, I guess, as long as it's okay with John."

"That's fine," John responded with a serious tone. "Just be careful. The desert's beautiful, but it can be dangerous. I swear, everything out there will either poke you, sting you, or bite you. Oh, and be especially careful of the jumping cacti."

"The what?" Dave asked in confusion.

"See that cactus over there? The one with the little balls on it that looks like a teddy bear? That's a jumping cactus."

Ashley's eyes grew wide. "Can they really jump?"

Sunshine laughed. "No, they can't jump, but if you get too close, it seems like they can. The needles catch easily in clothes and skin."

"We'll be careful," said Ashley.

"Make sure you take a jacket with you," Sunshine

suggested. "It'll be dark before long and, even though it's pleasant now, once the sun goes down, it'll cool off fast. By the time you get back, I'll have dinner ready." She smiled at them.

"Okay," they said in unison as they grabbed their jackets and stepped off the deck. They immediately headed toward a small path leading off into the desert.

"They seem like nice kids," remarked John.

"They are," said Sam, "but I'm a little concerned about them. They've both been very quiet and withdrawn since the night their mom died. Maybe I should go talk to them."

"Space and time," said Richard.

"Space and time?" Sam repeated, a little confused.

Richard leaned forward in his chair. "Don't crowd them. Give them the space and time they need to work things out in their minds. They've been through a lot in the last few days. It's going to take awhile for them to sort it all out. Don't worry. When they're ready to talk, they'll come to you."

"I guess you're right." Silently, though, parental concern for his kids still weighed heavily on his tired mind. He wrenched his hands.

Sunshine jumped up. "I'm going to start dinner so it will be ready in about an hour."

"I'll come help you," shot Lisa, "if you don't mind."

Jean rose. "I'll help, too."

Sunshine's green eye's beamed. "That's great. I'd love some help."

Once the women disappeared, Sam and Richard gave John a more detailed account of their trip.

A half-hour later, John shook his head. "Man, no wonder you're all so tired. You've been through a lot. We won't keep you up late tonight. As soon as we're done with dinner, you can go to sleep if you want to."

Dave and Ashley returned just in time for dinner. After eating and grabbing a quick shower, they pumped up their air mattresses, unrolled the sleeping bags, and settled in for the night.

Lisa took the couch, while Sam lay with the kids on the floor.

Just as Sam began drifting off, he heard Lisa say, "Good night, Sam, and thank you."

Quietly, he said, "Good night . . . and you're welcome."

Chapter 11

Morning dawned bright and clear. Thankful that John or Sunshine had set the automatic coffeepot the night before, Sam quietly poured a cup. He sat on the swing on the back deck to prevent waking anyone else.

A few minutes later, the door opened and Lisa came out with a steaming coffee cup.

"I hope I didn't wake you," he said.

"No, I've always been an early riser. Mornings are my favorite time of day." She sat on the swing next to him.

Interesting, he thought, *six empty chairs and she sits on the swing next to me.* "Mine, too, especially beautiful mornings like this. I looked at the thermometer on the wall and, according to it, it's a balmy fifty-five degrees out here. Back home in Wyoming, there's no way you could sit outside in December at 7:00 o'clock in the morning and wear just a light jacket." He realized he was babbling like a school boy on his first date. *I haven't felt like this since . . . my first date with Linda.* He realized he was starting to have feelings for Lisa. *Before this goes any further, I need to find out about her husband.*

She took a sip of coffee. "I know what you mean. This is more like a summer morning back home."

They sat without talking for a while.

While Sam enjoyed the play of light as the sun slowly rose over the desert, he thought about Lisa's husband, Shawn. *I wonder where he is? I wonder if he's alive?* Sam wasn't sure if he should bring it up or not, but curiosity got the better of him. "I'm curious about something," he mumbled.

"What?" she cautiously asked.

"You've mentioned your husband, Shawn, a couple of times. I was just wondering where he is."

Lisa took a deep breath and looked down at her coffee cup. When she looked up, her eyes were damp. "He died six months ago. He was thrown from his horse. The fall broke his neck."

The pain on her face warned Sam not to ask any more questions. On the one hand, he felt relieved. If he wanted to explore his feelings for her, he wouldn't have to deal with an ex-husband. On the other hand, he would have to compete with the love she obviously still had for Shawn. "That must have been hard . . . to lose him that way. I'm sorry."

"Thank you," she said with a silent tear running down her cheek. "Now, I have a question for you. What happened to your wife?"

He told her the whole story of the volcano erupting, deciding to leave their home, getting Ashley from Jenny's house, the traffic jam in Casper, the man shooting at them, one of the bullets hitting Linda, and how he had run the stop sign, almost hitting Richard and Jean. Tears had formed in his eyes by the time he finished. *I can't grieve for her now, not here.* He quickly wiped his eyes.

"I'm so sorry," she said. "That must have been a horrible experience, for all of you."

"It was." He took a big sip of coffee, swallowing hard to remove the lump in his throat. "That's why I'm so worried about my kids. They've been through so much in such a short time, I don't think it's all sunk in yet." He took another sip from his cup. "There's something else you should know about me and Linda. A week ago, we decided . . ."

The back door opened and Dave walked out.

"And speaking of the kids," Sam blurted, "here's one of them now. Good morning, Son, how are you today?"

Dave looked suspiciously from Sam to Lisa. "I'm fine, and it looks like you two are getting along just fine, too." He angrily stomped down the steps. "I'm going for a walk. I'll be back in a while."

Sam started to rise, but Lisa put her hand on his arm. "Remember," she said, "what Richard said last night: space and time. Maybe you should let him go for now."

"Yeah, I guess." Feeling helpless and way out of his element with how to handle the emotional issues, Sam dropped his head. "He probably just needs some time to sort things out."

Patting his knee, Lisa said, "It looks like everybody's up. Let's go in."

* * *

"Good morning," Sunshine said as Sam and Lisa walked inside. "I just put on a fresh pot of coffee, and I'll have breakfast ready in about thirty minutes."

"Thanks," Sam said. *I'm glad we ended up here. Sunshine and John really put themselves out for us.* On his way to pour another cup of coffee, he bumped into Jean.

Jean nearly dropped the bowl with the pancake mix. "This kitchen is too small for this many people," she said with frustration. "Why don't you men go in the living room and watch the news while we fix breakfast?"

"Sorry." Sam quickly poured his coffee and headed toward the living room.

John turned on the television and tuned it to a Phoenix station.

Naturally, there's a commercial playing, Sam thought impatiently as he set his cup on the coffee table and plopped down on the couch.

When the news anchorman finally appeared, he announced, "Our top story this morning is on the latest tragedy to befall this great nation of ours. It has been confirmed by a high-level government source that Mexico has, indeed, invaded the United States of America."

Stunned, Sam shot a look at Richard, who sat with his mouth open and eyes glued to the television.

"For more on this story, let's go to Monica Simpson, reporting live from Beale Air Force Base. . . . Monica?"

A shapely blond appeared on the screen in front of an Air Force office. "Yes, thank you, Fred. The White House Press Secretary confirmed, just moments ago, that Mexico has invaded the United States. He also said President Hamilton is expected to make a statement shortly."

"Monica, do you have any information on the invasion, like where the troops are coming across the border?"

"No, nothing concrete. There are rumors circulating among the members of the White House Press Core, but none of us want to speculate on them at this time."

Sam looked with disbelief from Richard to John. "Is this for real?"

"I think it is," Richard said somberly. "That's all we need right now."

John shook his head. "This isn't good. If Mexico is invading us, what are we going to do? We can't go north or east because of the volcano. Our only other options are west and northwest."

Sam interjected, "It looks like President Hamilton is going to make a statement. Let's see what she has to say."

President Hamilton, in a red business suit and wearing

her reading glasses, stepped up to the podium and looked straight into the camera. "Good morning. I'm sure you're all aware of the rumors going around about Mexican troops coming across our southern border. I regret to inform you that these rumors are true. At ten p.m. last night, Mexico launched an all-out invasion along the entire length of our southern border. I just left an emergency session with Congress. They voted and the decision was unanimous: we are now officially at war with Mexico. I have ordered all available troops to the frontline, and my advisors assure me that our military forces will be able to stop the advancement of the enemy troops and push them back across the border within two weeks.

"I spoke with Mexico's President earlier this morning. He informed me that he doesn't want to take the whole country, just everything below Interstate 40. He waited until the volcano crippled us, then attacked." Her voice rose with hostility. "Mexico thinks they can win a war against us. I have news for them. Even dealing with the aftermath of the volcano, we are still strong enough to repel this attack. We are the greatest nation on earth, and we will fight to the bitter end."

Pursing her lips, she scanned the audience. "On a personal note, I think Mexico's invasion is cowardly and immoral, and I promise you, the American people, that I will do everything in my power to protect you and your homes." She abruptly turned on her heels and stepped down from the podium. Her Secret Service detail and advisors scurried to keep up with her.

"I wish they would have given us more information," said Richard. "We know we're at war, but we don't know the location of the front, or if we should stay here."

"Be patient," John said, "somebody will tell us more about what's going on."

Sure enough, Paul Morrison, the White House Press Secretary, stepped up to the microphone. "As President Hamilton said, the Mexican army has invaded along our entire border, from San Diego, California, to Brownsville, Texas. The biggest push seems to be between Yuma, Arizona, and El Paso, Texas, where the Mexican army has moved as far as one hundred miles north of the border. For safety reasons, we want everyone living south of Interstate 40 to leave the area and go north, preferably into Northern California, Oregon, or Washington."

"You're talking millions of people," yelled one of the reporters. "Where are they supposed to stay when they get there?"

"We are in the process of setting up shelters," replied Paul. "Once these are full, the citizens living in these three states will have to take the remaining refugees into their homes."

"What about the people in southwestern hospitals and nursing homes?" called out another reporter. "And people that are homebound? Are you going to send people to help evacuate them?"

"Unfortunately, we don't have the resources to do that at this time. The hospitals are more than capable of evacuating their own. Everyone else will have to rely on family, friends, and neighbors."

"So, we're on our own," said the same reporter. "What happens to the people that won't or can't evacuate?"

"They don't have a choice," quipped Paul. "We're not *asking* them to leave. We're *ordering* them to leave."

"Let's see," said a third reporter, "if I remember right, it's only about two hundred miles north from Interstate 40 to the southern edge of the ash cloud. So, that means you want millions more people to flood into an area that's already overflowing with the refugees heading south and trying to escape the ash cloud. Do you really think the towns in that area can handle more people?"

"They don't have a choice," Paul snapped, clearly agitated. "We're at war. They'll have to do whatever they can in order to survive until we push the Mexican troops back across the border."

"Dave's back," Lisa shouted from the kitchen. "And breakfast is ready."

In a quiet tone, Richard said, "Listen, there's no sense in ruining breakfast for everybody. Why don't we wait until after we eat to tell them about this."

"I agree," Sam said, wrenching his hands. "Let's all have a nice leisurely meal. We can talk about this after we eat."

John nodded, turned off the television, and headed into the kitchen.

Setting a platter on the table, Sunshine asked cheerfully, "So, what's the latest news on the volcano?"

John responded casually, "Nothing much. Why don't we eat breakfast. Then, we'll go out on the deck and talk about it."

* * *

After breakfast, everyone gathered outside on the deck. The sun beamed brightly overhead.

Nervously, Sam looked at the others. When John gave him a nod, Sam swallowed hard and said, "Okay, we couldn't find any information on the volcano and the ash cloud. The news media is concentrating on another problem that's come up."

Jean frowned. "What could be more important than the ash cloud?"

"War," Richard said bluntly.

Jean stared at him with her mouth open.

Sam explained the details of the news reports and the President's speech about the invasion.

Fear, doubt, disbelief, shock, and anger crossed the faces of the listeners. In contrast, Dave's face filled with excitement.

As the news of war sank in, only the sound of a bird singing in a cactus could be heard.

Lisa was the first to get over her shock and break the silence. "Do you think the military can stop the Mexicans before they get this far north?"

John said, "I think they'll stop them long before they get here, and if they don't, we'll still have enough time to leave before they arrive. I've spent a lot of time out in this desert, and there's only a couple of ways the Mexican army can move their troops north. As long as we keep an eye on the situation, we'll be fine."

Sam was surprised at how calmly John was accepting the situation. *Of course, he's been in the military. He's been trained for war; we haven't.* "Like John says, we can always leave if they get too close. I vote we stay put and keep an eye on the situation for a couple of days. Our other option is to go on to my brother's in Oregon. Richard, what do you think?"

The big man pulled at the goatee on his chin. After getting a nod from scared-looking Jean, he said, "I agree we should stay, but I also think we need to be prepared to leave in a hurry if we have to. We should load everything we think we'll need into the vehicles, just in case we have to make a hasty retreat."

Wanting to make sure everybody had a say in the matter, Sam said, "Dave, what do you think?"

"I agree with Richard and John," Dave said. "Let's stay here and see what happens."

Sam looked at Ashley.

She sat on the swing with Sunshine's arm around her

shoulders. "I'll go along with whatever you guys decide."

He could tell she was scared. Anger coursed through him. *Damn, how much are we going to have to endure before things get back to normal?* "I have a bad feeling about this," he said to the group. "I think we should get out of here. Let's head up to Oregon."

"Remember the traffic coming down through Colorado?" Richard said. "I'm not sure we can go north, even if we want to."

"We have everything we need," John interjected, "even if they do attack."

Sam's gut told him to leave. Something bad was going to happen. In frustration, he said to John, "What are going to do for protection? How are we going to fight back? Do you have any weapons lying around?"

John smiled and gave Sunshine a wink. "I might. You three come with me. I want to show you something."

* * *

John led the men around the deck to the back of the house. He stopped in front of the small metal storage shed. He opened the door and the others followed him inside.

Sam estimated the shed flooring to be about ten square feet and the walls eight-feet tall. Storage benches sat along three sides.

John pulled on one of the benches. It swung away from the wall to reveal a trap door in the floor. He lifted the wooden door. To Sam's surprise, John exposed a steel security door with a number pad. John punched in an access code and the door slowly opened. A light snapped on, revealing a concrete-lined hole three-foot-square with a ladder on one side.

"Sweet," said Dave, looking as keyed-up as a kid on

Christmas morning.

"Wait until you see what's down there," said John excitedly.

At the bottom, Sam followed the others through a short tunnel, heading back under the house about ten feet. Before them appeared a solid steel door that looked like a door on a vault in a bank.

John spun the dial and entered a combination. He grabbed the handle and pulled. The door swung open and a light came on inside.

Sam looked around in amazement at the room in front of him. Twenty-by-twenty feet in size, it had been built with concrete walls and storage racks on three sides. A gun rack, ten-feet long and filled with upright rifles on both sides, sat in the middle of the room. The rifles included 22's, big-bore hunting rifles, shotguns, M-16's, and even a .50 caliber sniper rifle. Above the rifles, on cloth-covered boards, hung handguns from pegs. Next to them sat a section filled with knives and swords: everything from Swiss army knives to a ninja sword. The racks around the outer walls contained ammo boxes, duffle bags, and cardboard boxes.

"Well, what do you think?" asked John, grinning from ear to ear.

"Nothing like having your own personal armory," said Richard in admiration as his eyes scanned the weapons in the rifle case.

"This is awesome," Dave blurted, looking wide-eyed at the contents of the room.

Sam looked at Dave. "This really is awesome. Who would have thought that this was hidden under that beat-up old mobile home? No offense intended," he added, looking quickly at John.

"None taken. I made the mobile home look beat-up and trashy on purpose, to discourage people from snooping around."

"What's in the duffle bags?" Dave asked.

"Survival gear. Everything from extra clothes to MREs, night-vision goggles, gas masks, everything you would need to survive in case of an emergency."

Richard walked to a shelf with four large boxes. After reading the label, he asked John, "Are you kidding me? Are these real?"

"You bet they're real. You might say I believe in being prepared."

"What are they?" Dave asked eagerly, stepping next to Richard.

"Handheld rocket launchers," said Richard, "flame throwers, and grenades."

"Well," Sam remarked, "I've got to admit, you're definitely prepared for a war. But I've got to ask, why did you do this?"

"You might say it's a hobby of mine. I've always been interested in guns and weapons, in general. I have a good friend that's an armory-supply sergeant in the army. You wouldn't believe what he's offered to sell me. I started collecting. When we moved out here, I wanted someplace secure to store them, someplace safer than under my bed, so I built this room before the contractor placed the mobile home on top. He didn't have a clue it was here, by the way."

"How thick are the walls?" Sam asked.

"Two feet of steel-reinforced concrete," John proudly stated. "Strong enough to take a hit from almost anything."

"Where does that ladder go, John?" Dave asked, pointing to a ladder going up to a closed trap door in the ceiling at the end of the room.

"That one comes out in the master bedroom closet. I wanted to be able to access this room from the house, too, but I won't use it unless I have to."

"Why not?" Dave questioned.

"Because it's a smaller entrance hole. And it isn't as hidden as well as the outer entrance."

Sam walked to a topographical map hanging on the wall. "Is this a map of this area?"

John started to reply, but was interrupted by Lisa's faint voice from above.

"Sam . . . Sam, could you come up here for a minute? We have a small problem."

He yelled up to her, "Yeah, I'll be right up. We're done down here anyway." Turning to Richard and John, he murmured, "Now what?" He headed toward the vault door.

"Go ahead," said John. "We'll be right up."

When he got to the top of the ladder, he saw Lisa, Jean, and Ashley standing outside the storage shed. All looked unhappy.

"Okay, so what's wrong now?"

Lisa started to explain. "Well, I asked Ashley . . . "

"She didn't *ask* me," Ashley broke in. "She *told* me. She's not my mom and she has no right to . . . "

"Stop right there, young lady," Sam barked. He decided, right then-and-there, it was time to talk to the kids about everything that had happened since the volcano had erupted. "Dave," he yelled into the shed.

"Yeah, Dad?" Dave said casually as he walked out of the shed.

"Dave, Ashley, let's go for a walk. I think there's some things we need to talk about."

Lisa took a step forward. "Sam, I . . . "

"Don't . . . " He held up his hand. "Just . . . let me handle this. Okay?"

Putting her hands up, she backed away. "Okay, okay."

* * *

Sam led the kids up the trail behind the house to a large flat rock. As Dave and Ashley sat down, he said firmly, "Okay, who wants to go first?"

Both stared at the ground. Ashley fidgeted with the hem of her t-shirt.

"Well, then, I guess I'll start," Sam said with a sigh. "Dave, you seem like you're mad at me for some reason. What's going on?"

"I'm not sure I'm ready to talk about it."

Sam sighed again and softened his voice. "Listen, kids, a lot has happened to us in the last week. I think it will help all of us to talk about it."

Dave glanced at Ashley, then turned back at Sam. "We're upset because of Lisa."

Sam frowned in confusion. "Lisa? Why? What did she do?"

"Because of the way you two look at each other," he blurted with vehemence. Abruptly, his shoulders sagged. His eyes dropped. "I mean . . . Mom's only . . . "

"I think I know what's wrong." Sam broke in. "You're mad because you think there's something going on between me and Lisa, right?"

They both nodded, still looking at the ground.

"And, you think I'm being unfaithful to your mom, right?"

They nodded again. This time, they both looked up sheepishly.

Sam looked at Ashley. "And, you think I'm already trying to replace her?" He let out a long sigh and sat down on the rock between them. "Okay, I guess it's time I told you some things that you don't know about me and your mom. For the last few years, our marriage had been on shaky ground. I found out six months ago that your mom was seeing someone else." He paused to let this news sink in.

"Mom was having an affair?" Dave asked skeptically.

"I don't believe it," Ashley stated.

He knew the next bit of news would be the hardest for them to accept. "We were both unhappy and wanted out of the marriage, so last week, we decided to file for divorce."

They stared at him, shock and anger clearly showing on their faces.

"We were going to tell you the night the volcano erupted, but we never got the chance. And, as far as Lisa and I go, there isn't anything going on between us. I don't know if there ever will be. She's a little too high-strung and bitchy for me."

"Who was Mom seeing?" Dave asked looking Sam in the eye.

"Truthfully, I don't know. I didn't want to know." Sam felt a flash of anger. *Dammit, Linda, I didn't want to tell the kids this and deal with it by myself.* Then, he felt guilty, knowing it wasn't her fault she was killed. "Listen," he quietly said, "I'm really sorry your mom didn't make it. I still love her and always will."

Trying not to cry, Ashley blurted, "There's nothing going on between you and Lisa?"

"No, absolutely not," Sam replied staunchly. "Right now, there are too many other things going on to even think about getting involved in a relationship. Are you mad because you think Lisa is trying to be a mother figure? Or, are you mad that your mom died and Lisa didn't, so you're taking your anger out on Lisa?"

"I see what you mean, Dad," she said, her bottom lip quivering and tears running down her cheeks. "You're right. I am mad that Mom died and Lisa didn't. It's not fair."

He reached his arms around her and she fell sobbing into his chest. "I'm so sorry, Ash. Everything that's happened to us in the last week has been unfair, but life's not always fair. When life deals us a bad hand, all we can do is the best we can. We have to deal with it and move on."

In a tone of resignation, Dave said, "You're right. I'm sorry I've been such an ass lately."

Sam let go of Ashley. "That's okay, Son. Like I said, we just need to deal with everything that's happened and try to move on. I promise you, as soon as we can, we'll head for Uncle Jerry's in Oregon where we can make a new home. So, are we good now?"

"Yeah, Dad, we're good."

"I'm sorry, too, Dad," Ashley said. "I just miss Mom so much."

"I know, Honey, we all do. Are you okay with everything now?"

"No, but I'll work on it," she admitted.

"Okay. Well, if we're done talking, why don't we head back and help get ready for the next disruption in our lives." Sam chuckled and stood up, dusting off his pants.

"I have a question about that," said Ashley, jumping off the rock.

"Sure, Honey, shoot."

She cocked her head to the side. "That's just it, will I have to shoot any Mexicans when they get here?"

He laughed. "No, Sweetheart. I promise, I'll make sure you don't have to shoot anybody. Hell, I doubt we'll even see any Mexicans. We'll be long gone before they get here."

* * *

Unfortunately, the wheel of fate was about to deal them a bad hand. Sam had no idea that, within days, some of them would end up performing actions they would have never dreamed of doing, including killing people.

Part II

The Mexicans

Chapter 12

Coming out of a deep sleep, Sam felt someone shaking his shoulder.

"Wake up, I think we may have a problem," said John.

"What's wrong?" Sam rubbed his eyes, trying to wake up. "Is something wrong with Dave or Ashley?"

"No, they're fine, but I think the Mexican army's here."

A surge of adrenaline rushed through Sam. He jolted awake. "What do you mean by *here*? Are they outside?" He threw off the covers and sat up.

"Not yet, but I think they're a lot closer than we thought, maybe as close as a couple of miles."

Sam glanced at the clock: six a.m. *Well, I guess it's time to get up anyway.* "Do you think we should wake everybody up," he asked as he pulled on his pants.

"Definitely," John replied. "We need to find out how close they are and figure out what we want to do. If they're that close, we could be in big trouble."

Five minutes later, Sam walked into the kitchen and took the cup of coffee that Sunshine offered him. Dave and Ashley, rubbing sleep out of their eyes, entered the kitchen behind him. John, Richard, and Jean were sitting at the table.

Peering out the window, everything seemed normal to Sam. "Okay, John, what makes you think the Mexicans are so close?"

"Listen, can't you hear it?"

Sam listened. He heard faint booms that sounded like fireworks. His heart skipped a beat. "Is that artillery?" he uttered in disbelief.

"Yes," responded John, "and if you go outside, you can also hear gunfire."

"So, they moved a lot further north than we had expected," gulped Sam. His hands began to shake. He had never fought in a war and didn't know if he could handle something like this. He feared for his life and the welfare of his kids.

Richard, seeming totally calm in the face of pending disaster, asked, "Can you tell how far south of us they are?"

"Actually, they're north of us." John got up and dumped his coffee in the sink. "I'm afraid we're behind enemy lines."

Sam felt the blood drain from his face. He looked at the range of emotions on the faces in the room: shock, disbelief, and anger. *This sucks. How in the hell did this happen? No . . . how in the hell did this happen so fast? It's only been two days since we heard about the invasion.* He wished he'd taken the kids and left for Oregon the previous day while they still had the chance to get through. Now, he was stuck with no way out. Trying to keep his voice from trembling, he asked, "Okay, so now what do we do? Does anybody have any suggestions?"

"I do," said Richard, gripping his cup tightly. "I think we need to get the hell out of here as fast as possible. John, do you know any dirt roads that we can take to avoid running into the fighting?"

"Sure, I think . . . it depends on where the front lines are." He leaned against the counter and crossed his arms. "And the only way to find out is to go out and take a look."

The thought made Sam cringe. *What if we don't get back?*

"How could this have happened?" said Lisa in total dismay. "How did they get past us? You would think that we would've heard something, with an army passing by outside."

"Not necessarily," said John, shaking his head. "There are only two main roads going north in this area. Arizona 95 is west of here about ten miles. On the other side of the lake is California 95. They're both far enough away that an army could have moved up either one and we'd have never known."

Dave piped up. "But, wouldn't our army be trying to stop them? Wouldn't we hear the fighting? We can hear it now."

John stood at the end of the table and rubbed his neck. "That's because the fighting we hear now is a lot closer than either one of those roads, with no mountain in between. I'm betting the fighting we're hearing is taking place on I-40, which is only five miles from here.

"Since I know the area, I should be the one to do a recon mission and determine the safest route out of here. But, I would like someone to ride along with me and act as a lookout. Any volunteers?"

"I'll go," Dave offered enthusiastically, almost coming out of his seat.

"I don't think so," Sam said, giving him a disapproving glare.

"Why not?" He looked at Sam with consternation, as though he was being mistreated.

"Because it could be dangerous. I'll go. Besides, I need you to stay here and make sure everything's ready to go. We may come back in a hurry and, if we come flying in here with the whole Mexican army on our asses, I want everything and everybody ready to go in an instant. We may not have time to do anything but jump in the truck and get out of here. Can you do that for me,

Dave?"

Dave slumped back in his seat like a balloon deflating. "Sure, no problem. I'll make sure we're ready."

"We'll be in radio contact with them, at least part of the time," stated John to Sam. "There's a CB in the house and one in the Jeep. Before we go, let's go down to the vault and get some guns. We don't want to go out there unprotected."

Sam jumped up, nervous energy coursing through his body. "Good idea. We probably should bring some up for everybody else while we're at it." *Just in case,* he thought.

"Can I pick mine out?" Dave asked.

"Sure," John said, "as long as it's okay with your dad."

Sam looked around the room. "Does anybody else want to pick out their own?"

With disgust, Jean said, "I don't want one. I don't know the first thing about guns and I don't want to learn."

"Same here," Sunshine declared. "We'll stay up here and start breakfast."

The look on their faces told Sam it would be useless to argue with them. Shrugging his shoulders, he said, "Okay, if that's how you feel, that's fine with me."

John and Richard both gave him a "smart man" look.

Sam thought, *Hey, I was married long enough to know when not to argue with a woman.*

* * *

Leaving Jean and Sunshine upstairs, Sam and the others went outside and down to the gun vault to pick out their guns.

In keeping with his military background, John chose

an M-16 and a 1911 Colt 45 ACP.

Sam picked up a lever-action Winchester 30-30 with a Bushnell 3x10 scope. "This will do me just fine," he said as he worked the lever, making sure the rifle was unloaded.

"What about a pistol?" John asked.

"I've got my .40 cal. Glock upstairs," Sam responded. "I'll use *it*."

"Can I use this one?" Dave asked, holding up a .50 cal. Desert Eagle pistol.

"No," said John. "That's not a good personal defense weapon. You need something you can shoot fast and not worry about tearing your arm off every time you pull the trigger." He took the pistol from Dave and put it back on its hook. "Why don't you take this one instead." He held out a Berretta 9-MM.

Sheepishly, Dave said, "Yeah I guess it does make sense to use a gun that you can control if somebody's trying to kill you." He reached out to take the Berretta from John.

"I assume you know how to use it?" John asked before he released it.

Sam had been watching. "Don't worry, he and Ashley have both taken gun-safety courses, and I've personally made sure they both know how to handle them."

"Yeah, he used to take us out shooting all the time back home," Ashley said. "The four of us used to . . ." Her voice trailed off and she looked at the floor.

Sam, sharing her pain, approached her and put his arm around her. "I miss her, too, Ash." He hugged her and kissed the top of her head. "So, what do you think of this one for you?" He picked up a double-action Colt 38 Special and held it out to her.

She looked doubtfully at him. "Do I need one? I thought you said I wouldn't have to shoot anybody?"

"Don't worry, you probably won't have to use it, but I want you to have it just in case."

She took it and pushed the button on the side of the frame, flipping open the cylinder like it was an everyday occurrence. "It's not loaded," she pointed out to John.

"Don't worry, I have plenty of ammunition. Come on, I'll get you some."

Richard's voice boomed out. "I think I'll take this one, if it's okay with you John." He held up a stainless-steel Ruger Super Blackhawk .44 mag.

"Sure, a big man needs a big gun." John chuckled as he and Ashley walked off to get the ammo.

"What about you, Lisa?" Sam asked. "What do you want?"

"I have my shotgun and my pistol. I don't need anything else."

"That's right, you're pretty good with that shotgun." He winked at her and was surprised to see her face flush bright red.

"Shush, I don't want anybody else to know," she whispered, tipping her head in the direction of Ashley.

Sam nodded in understanding, glad that Lisa and Ashley were trying to get along.

"Okay, does everybody have ammo and holsters?" John asked.

Getting nods from everyone, he said, "Good, then Sam and I can hit the road."

* * *

Back upstairs, John gathered everyone in the living room. "Okay, everybody, listen up. I want you to keep your guns handy at all times. We have no idea what might happen in the next few hours or days, and I think it would be best to be prepared." Getting somber nods of agreement all around, he looked at Sam. "Are you ready?"

"As ready as I'll ever be," he replied, wiping his sweaty hands on his pants.

They climbed into John's Jeep and headed down the road. A half-mile later, John turned onto a small road that was nothing more than two tire tracks leading north up a steep hill.

"This small mountain range is called the Buck Mountains," John said, pointing to the surrounding hills. "There's an old mine up here and, from the top, we'll be able to see the whole valley, along with the freeway. Hopefully, we'll get a pretty good idea of what's going on around us."

The Jeep bounced over a rock, tossing Sam half out of his seat.

John smiled. "You know, if you put on your seat belt, it will keep you in your seat."

"I didn't think about that. I didn't think there was a chance of getting in a wreck out here, so I didn't put it on." He hastily fastened his seat belt.

Two miles later, after climbing to within fifty feet of the top a steep hill, John pulled over and parked. "Let's walk from here. We don't want anybody to see us drive over the top. And no loud voices. Whispers only."

Sam nodded as he unlocked his seatbelt and got out. The rising sun was bathing the desert in a soft, mellow light, and he took just a moment to enjoy the view before following John up the road.

When they were almost to the top, John stopped. "Can you hear that?" he quietly asked, cocking his head to the side.

Sam turned his head from side to side, listening intently. Whispering back, he said, "No, I don't hear anything."

"That's the problem. The fighting's stopped. Wait here. I'll be right back." With puzzlement and worry etched on his face, John went down on his belly and crawled to the crest of the hill. He stayed still for a minute, then slowly crawled forward until Sam lost sight of him.

If there aren't any sounds of fighting, that means somebody has won. I hope to god it was our side. He looked around nervously, half expecting a hoard of Mexican soldiers to come charging over the hill. Apprehension about what might be happening over the hill and at the trailer forced him to look for something else to occupy his mind. He double-checked his guns to make sure they were loaded, then leaned the rifle against a rock and sat down.

He watched a wary lizard run from rock to rock. "I know how you feel, little guy," he whispered, sending the lizard scurrying for cover. "I'm worried about getting eaten alive, too."

A slight breeze started blowing, bringing with it a low rumbling noise.

Sam listened intently, trying to figure out what was hearing.

Ten minutes later, John came crawling back, slightly out of breath. "When you crawl up to the top, make sure you have a brush or something in front of you ok?"

"Alright. Why? What's over there?" Sam asked, suddenly scared by John's demeanor and the look on his face.

"You've got to see it to believe it," he said quickly, crawling away.

Crawling on his hands and knees, Sam almost reached the top of the hill when he realized the noise he had been hearing was growing louder. *What the hell is that?* The closer he got, the louder the rumble sounded. He crawled behind a small mesquite bush some five feet to the right of John and peered over the steep slope to the valley below.

The valley ran a good ten miles from east to west and expanded to at least five miles across. The Mexican army, spread out from the base of Sam's hill to the freeway two miles away, covered most of that area with Jeeps, Hummers, tanks, troop transporters, artillery, helicopters, and hoards of soldiers.

Further away, Sam saw two cargo planes, sitting on the freeway. Chills ran down his spine as he estimated there were at least ten thousand soldiers on the valley floor. Looking at John, he whispered, "You've got to be shitting me. That looks like half the Mexican army down there. Where's our army? I don't see any American troops anywhere. This is not good."

"No, it isn't good," John replied flatly. "I think they kicked the shit out of our troops."

"So, what about a route out of here? Do you see any way to get around that army without getting caught?" Sam looked at the mountains, suddenly feeling trapped.

"That's the bad news: no, I don't. Unfortunately, as you can see, the way the land lies here, we're between two mountain ranges that run north to south, and there are no roads over either one. So that limits our movements to the north," he said pointing at the valley floor, "which is obviously not an option, nor south, which will put us deeper into enemy territory."

Frustrated and worried about the kids, Sam snapped, "Okay, so how far south are we going to have to go to get around these guys?"

"That brings up another problem. We can only go so far. About thirty miles south of here lies the Bill Williams River, and there's only one road that crosses it: Planet Ranch Road. It's private property with fences and locked gates. If we're lucky, there won't be anybody around and we can cross it, then head northwest."

"I would think that, under the circumstances, the owners wouldn't care if we crossed, would they?"

"It's not the owners I'm worried about. If whoever is in charge of this army is smart, they'll have somebody there to catch people like us."

With a sigh, Sam said, "Well, if that's our only option, then that's what we have to do. When we get close, we can check it out and see if it's safe. If not, we'll have to figure something else out." His eyes roamed across the valley, still not quite believing the assemblage of soldiers, vehicles, and weapons he was seeing.

"Let's get out of here before somebody see's us," John said, carefully scooting backwards down the hill.

In the Jeep, heading back to the trailer, Sam asked, "So, after we get over this river, where are we going?"

"With any luck at all, we'll find a way past the Mexican army and get back to U.S.-controlled ground." John guided the Jeep around a wicked hole in the road.

A burst of static came out of the CB radio. "Dad . . . can you hear me? It's Ashley." Before Sam could pick up the mike, she added, her voice trembling, "If you can hear me, please answer. We have a major problem here." It sounded like she was crying.

This has to be an emergency. Sam grabbed the mike. "What's wrong, Ash?"

"Dad," she said in a rush. "Thank God, you answered. Where are you? How soon can you get here?"

"Slow down, Honey, and tell me what's wrong." Sam envisioned a platoon of Mexican soldiers surrounding the trailer.

"About five minutes ago, a Jeep full of Mexican soldiers pulled up in front of the house, and they're demanding that we come out and surrender."

Sam felt like he had been punched in the gut. He looked at John. "How fast can you get us to your place?"

"Five minutes tops, but . . . "

Cutting John off, Sam pushed the talk button. "Ash, we'll be there in five minutes." *And I hope we're not four minutes too late.*

"Okay, just hurry. We're all scared. We don't know what to do."

"Come on, let's go," Sam said, buckling up his seat belt.

"We need to think about this for a minute," John said.

"We may not have a minute," Sam sternly countered. "Let's go."

"Hey, I realize you're worried about your kids, but I don't want to go waltzing in there without knowing what we're walking into and take the chance of getting captured or killed. What good would we be to them then? Maybe we can come up with a plan to try to take them by surprise or something."

Realizing John was right, Sam said, "Yeah, you're probably right."

John took the CB mike from Sam. "Ashley, this is John. I need you to tell me exactly what the situation is. How many soldiers are there? Where are they? Are all of you still in the house?"

"There're four soldiers and they're all standing next to their Jeep. We're all in the house."

"Okay, I want you to go get Richard. Tell him I need to talk to him."

"Alright, hang on a sec, and I'll get him."

Sam thought she didn't sound as upset as she had earlier. "What are you thinking? Do you have a plan of some kind?"

"Possibly, but I need to talk to Richard before I'll know for sure." John nervously tapped the mike on his leg.

Richard's voice boomed over the speaker. "John, it's Richard. Are you there?"

"Yeah, Richard I'm here. Listen, I need to know the situation there. How serious is it?"

"Very serious, I'm afraid. I've been trying to talk to the soldier in charge, a Major Sanchez. He isn't being very cooperative. He says, if we don't surrender in the next five minutes, he'll come in and take us by force, which he said he would rather not do, since it would be a shame if the women got killed before he and his men could *enjoy* them."

Sam didn't miss the emphasis on *enjoy*.

"Okay," John replied, "give me a minute to come up with a plan." He looked at Sam. "You heard Richard. You know what's going to happen if we don't do something to save our friends and family. What I want to know is, are you willing . . . " He paused. "No, let me rephrase that. When the time comes, can you kill someone to save your kids?"

Sam leaned his head back on the headrest and took a deep breath. His heart pounded in his chest. "I know what you're asking. We go through life, saying, 'Man, I'd kill for this or that.' But, they're only words. This is the real thing." He stayed quiet for a moment, contemplating John's question. He sat up straight, took a deep breath, and looked John in the eye. "Yes, I can. I already lost my wife to some asshole with a gun. I'm not going to lose either one of my kids. Whatever you need me to do, I'll do it. You can count on me."

John studied him for a few seconds, as if he was trying to decide if Sam was really as confident and self-assured as he seemed. Making his decision, he put the mike to his mouth. "Richard, are you there?"

Richard replied immediately. "Yeah, go ahead."

"Who's there with you? Anybody? Or can you talk freely?"

"There's nobody close enough to hear what we're saying. What's up?"

"Here's the deal: the situation there could get violent. What I need to know from you is: if you need to, in order to protect the life of your wife, can you kill someone?"

"Hell, yeah," he bellowed. In a quieter tone, he said, "Listen, I may be a doctor, but that doesn't mean I'm against violence. If you're worried about me not being able to blow some guy away, you can stop worrying. I'll do what I need to do."

"Good, that's what I needed to know. Now, here's my plan," he said into the mike as he looked at Sam. "We pull up to the house like we don't know there's a war going on. When we get out of the Jeep, we each take out one of the soldiers. Richard, you can take one out from inside, then either Sam or I will take the last one. What do you think?"

"Don't worry about things on this end," Richard said with confidence. "We'll take care of everything."

As John put the radio down, Sam said doubtingly, "That's kind of simple, isn't it?"

"Haven't you ever heard of K.I.S.S.: Keep It Simple Stupid. The more complex a plan is, the more that can go wrong. Most of the time, a simple plan works better than a elaborate, complex one."

"That's true. Okay, it sounds good to me. Now, let's get over there before Major Sanchez gets a wild hair up his ass and decides to storm the house and have his way with our women." Determined to protect his kids, no matter what, Sam pulled out his gun.

Chapter 13

When John pulled up in the driveway, Sam saw the four soldiers standing in front of a Jeep.

At the sound of John's vehicle, they moved to the back of the Jeep with their rifles slung over their shoulders.

Good, they don't look like they're on alert, Sam thought.

"Follow my lead," John said calmly as he slid out his handgun and racked the slide, chambering a round. "Stay behind your door until we're ready to dance. I'll take the one on the far left. You take the one on the far right. Keep your gun out of sight until I tell you."

Sam couldn't believe John's calmness, while his own stomach flip-flopped in his belly. His dry mouth made it hard to swallow, let alone speak. He just nodded.

As they opened their doors and exited the Jeep, John said, "*Hola, Amigos,* how's your mama?"

The soldiers looked at each other in bewilderment as they shook their heads.

John calmly said, "Now." He lifted his gun and fired, catching everyone, Sam included, completely off-guard.

It took several seconds for Sam to react. The soldier he was supposed to shoot already had his rifle off his shoulder and was lining it up on him. Unwilling to look at the soldier's face, Sam concentrated on a button in the center of the man's chest. He whipped his pistol up and shot twice, hitting his guy both times. He turned to look for another target, but the soldiers were all on the ground . . . dead.

"Are you okay?" John asked as he approached Sam. "You don't look so good. You're as white as a ghost." He gently took the pistol from Sam's shaking hands.

"Um . . . yeah . . . I think . . . I need to sit down for a minute." Feeling sick to his stomach, Sam lowered himself to the ground and leaned back on the front tire of the Jeep.

Ashley came out of the house. Seeing him on the ground, she panicked, apparently thinking he had been shot, too. "Daddy, are you okay?" she cried out, running to him and kneeling by his side.

"I'm fine, Ash," he said weakly. "I didn't think shooting someone would affect me this way." He reached out and gave her hand a squeeze. He refused to look at the soldiers again as John checked them to make sure they were dead.

"I'm glad it affected you that way," said Richard as he stood behind Ashley and looked a little shaken himself. "Killing another human being *should* be a traumatic experience. If it wasn't, think how many people would kill someone else for any mundane reason. It's when killing doesn't bother you that you have to worry."

"Well, I'm glad it's over, and I hope I never have to do it again." Sam laid his head back and closed his eyes to try to calm his shattered nerves.

John said to Sam, "Why don't you stay where you are and rest for a little bit. Richard and I will take care of the mess we made."

"I'll help you," Dave said enthusiastically.

Sam opened one eye and looked at Dave. He hazily wondered why Dave was so excited to help take care of the dead soldiers. But Sam's mind wasn't working right. He let it go until later. "I think I want to go in the house and lay down for a minute." Sam tried to stand up, but his weakness prevented him from getting to his feet.

Sunshine came to his side. "Here, let me help you so you don't fall down." Taking hold of his arm, she tried pulling him to his feet.

Lisa came up on his other side and helped heft him to his feet.

The motion of standing up caused Sam's stomach to churn. He put his hands on his belly and hoped to make it into the bathroom before he heaved. "Thanks, I'm sorry I . . . oh-oh, I think I'm going to . . . " He pushed Lisa and Sunshine away as he leaned over and threw up. Fortunately, all he had in his stomach was the morning's coffee. He wiped his mouth with the back of his hand. "Sorry about that. I was hoping to make it inside."

"Don't worry about it," Sunshine said kindly.

"It's a natural reaction," added Lisa, taking his arm again. "I would rather have it affect you this way than to not have it affect you at all. I feel a little bit sick myself, and I didn't shoot anybody." She forced a laugh.

Inside, Lisa and Sunshine helped Sam onto the couch.

When they stepped away, Ashley sat down on the edge of the couch. "Is there anything I can do for you, Dad?" she asked quietly. She looked pale.

Sam realized the whole experience was traumatic for her, too. "Yeah, there is. Just sit with me." He took her hand and held it.

She rubbed the back of his hand. "Thanks for . . . um, you know, doing what you did out there."

"You're welcome. Why don't you turn on the T.V. and let's see if we can find out the latest news on the invasion. Maybe they'll say something about the volcano. We haven't heard anything about it in a while." He closed his eyes, only to see, again and again, the soldier he had shot falling backwards.

* * *

An hour later, Sam heard the men enter the house. He heard Dave's voice next to him.

"How are you feeling, Dad?" Dave gently laid his hand on Sam's arm.

Sam opened one eye, squinting in the harsh sunlight streaming in from the window. Clearing his throat, he said, "Better, I think. But I could use something to drink."

"I'll get you something. What do you want? Bourbon, vodka, or whiskey," Dave joked.

"Funny," said Sam, feeling nauseated at the thought. "Orange juice or Apple juice, if they have any." He sat up and smoothed down his hair as Ashley settled next to him.

"One juice coming right up," announced Dave as he walked to the kitchen.

The scent of bacon, eggs, and pancakes permeated the house. It smell good at first, then Sam's stomach gave a slight heave. He decided to try the juice now and, maybe, the food later.

John and Richard sat down in the recliners across the room.

Richard said, "As soon as we're done eating breakfast, we're leaving. It won't be long before those soldiers are missed. We need to be as far from here as we can get."

"That's right," John agreed. "They're going to scour this whole area. We did what we could, but there's not a lot of places to hide a Jeep and four dead bodies in the open desert." He shrugged.

Dave returned with a glass of orange juice. He glanced at the T.V. as he walked into the room. "Is there any new news on the war or the volcano and ash cloud?"

"I'm not sure," Sam said as he took the orange juice into his mildly shaking hands. "I wasn't really paying all that much attention."

"I was," offered Ashley.

Richard looked at her expectantly. When she didn't elaborate, he said bluntly, "Well, spit it out, girl. What did they say?"

"Um . . . let's see. The anchorman said that our army is having 'logistic' problems moving their troops around, and they're asking the people of America to step up and help. He said the people need to take up arms and help fight off the enemy."

John laughed. "In other words, the army's getting it's ass kicked and they need us, the people, to step in and save them." He looked at Sam. "Now, I know why we didn't see any of our troops in that valley this morning."

Sam nodded, his mind reeling with the implications of a government that couldn't protect its citizens. He realized that he and his kids would, more than likely, have to fight for their lives before this whole ordeal was over. *Damn, I don't want my kids to go through what I just did. There's got to be some way to get out of here and to Oregon without fighting and killing.*

Breaking into his thoughts, Dave said, "Did they say anything about the volcano?"

Ashley slowly nodded her head yes. "The good news is, the ash cloud has now moved as far east as it's going to go. The bad news is, the jet stream changed direction and the ash cloud is now moving towards the south and west areas of the country."

"We're in the southwest," blurted Dave.

"Yes, we are," admitted Sam. *Shit, that's all we need.* The orange juice had helped settle his stomach and got rid of his weakness. Now, he began to feel restless. Rising, he crossed the room and looked out the sliding-door window that led to the deck.

John asked, "Ashley, did they say how far southwest they expect it to go? And how long it will keep heading in this direction?"

Tears formed in her eyes. "According to their predictions, they say it's going to go as far west as San Diego and as far south as the Gulf of Mexico. That's why they said south and west, because it is going to cover such a wide area."

"How long before it gets here?" Richard asked, worry plainly showing on his broad, dark face.

"Sometime tomorrow. They said it's approaching Las Vegas now."

"What's approaching Vegas?" demanded Jean as she entered the living room, followed by Sunshine and Lisa. "And what's it got to do with us?"

"The ash cloud from the volcano," stated John.

"Good, I'm glad you're here," said Richard as he stood up, "Everybody needs to hear this."

Sam turned around and leaned against the sliding door to listen to the conversation.

Jean and Sunshine sat on the couch, one on each side of Ashley. Sunshine gave Ashley's leg a squeeze, silently telling her everything was going to be okay.

Richard clasped his hands behind his back and slowly paced the room like a college professor giving a lecture. "Apparently, the volcanic ash is going to catch up with us. This ash is made up of, among other things, silica. If you breath in the ash, the silica settles in your lungs and you die from asphyxiation. We'll need to be very careful not to breath any of it."

"It will cause breathing problems for the vehicles, also," said John.

Sam saw the puzzled looks on the faces of Jean and Sunshine.

John continued with an explanation. "A carburetor mixes the gasoline and air needed for combustion. If the ash blocks the air filter, the carburetor won't be able to get the air it needs, and the gasoline won't burn."

"So, it will be like it's flooded," said Ashley. "Like you did to the four-wheeler that time, right, Dad?"

"That's right," Sam said. *So, how in the hell are we supposed to get away from here now? We can't walk out. this really screws things up with trying to escape the Mexican soldiers.*

"Why don't we stay here?" Dave eagerly suggested. "If we ration it, we should have enough food to last for quite a while." His eyes flared wide, his cheeks flushed, and his hands started shaking.

Damn, thought Sam, watching the change in Dave, *he's getting unduly excited. Time for another adrenaline fix. I need to talk to him and put a stop to this.*

"What if the patrol they send out to look for their missing soldiers comes here?" Jean asked. "Then what do we do?"

Dave surged ahead. "We can hide in the gun vault and only come out long enough to fix food and use the bathroom. The entrances are hidden pretty good. I don't think they'll find them. They'll probably just do a quick check of the house and then leave."

Sunshine shook her head. "I, for one, don't want to be cooped up in that vault for the next week."

John put up his hands. "No, hang on a minute, that's actually not a bad idea. The Mexicans are going to have the same problems with their vehicles as we do. Once the ash hits, it will severely limit their movements, so we won't need to stay below that long. Twenty-four hours, tops."

Sam rubbed his chin thoughtfully. "I don't know if I like the idea of being down there with no way out. What happens if the soldiers search the place and they *do* find the entrance? We'll be sitting ducks down there."

Lisa nodded fervently. "I agree with Sam. If they find the entrance, there's no way out. I think we'd better figure out something else."

John and Sunshine looked at each other. She nodded her head and gave him an it's-okay look.

John cleared his throat. "Um, there's a couple of things I didn't tell you about the vault."

Everybody stared at him, expecting bad news.

He looked sheepishly around the room. "What I didn't tell you was that the vault is completely self-contained. There are solar panels on the roof of the trailer for power. The ventilation system for both the vault and the living quarters has an air scrubber to remove carbon dioxide."

"Living quarters?" exclaimed Sam, looking around in surprise.

John held up a hand, gesturing for Sam to wait until he was done talking. "It's got independent piping for the plumbing, which comes straight from the well. There's a two-year supply of food for two people. And, best of all, there's a hidden escape tunnel that comes out about a hundred yards behind the house."

"So, how come you didn't tell us about this stuff before?" said Dave, acting a little miffed.

"Because," he bluntly replied, "I didn't think you needed to know about it."

"So, how big is this living area?" Richard asked.

"It's the same size as the vault: twenty-by-twenty, four-hundred-square-feet."

Estimating how all this would work out, Sam said, "The two rooms together, then, are around eight-hundred-square-feet, about the size of a small apartment."

"Yeah, but remember, it was only built for two people. That means there are only two cots."

Ashley piped up with, "That's okay. I'm sure we can make it work if we need to. Can't we, Dad?"

"Sure, especially with all the camping equipment we have out in the truck."

John shot him a look of surprise. "You have camping equipment with you?"

"Yeah, when we left home, right after the earthquake hit, I wasn't sure where we were going or what we would need, so I threw in everything I could think of."

"Well, that's good. I'm sure we can . . . "

Suddenly, the roar of a helicopter filled the room. The pictures shook on the walls.

A shiver ran up Sam's spine. The helicopter had to be right above the roof of the house.

"Oh, oh," said Ashley, her eyes wide with terror. "I think they're here looking for the missing soldiers already."

Sunshine, looking frightened herself, put her arms around Ashley and pulled her close.

"Shit," John said, jumping up and running to the plate-glass window. He cautiously peered out through the blinds.

"What do you think? Is it the Mexicans?" asked Dave excitedly.

"I think we're in deep shit," John muttered as he moved away from the window and opened the blinds.

Sam watched the line of military vehicles coming up the main road. His mouth went dry.

Chapter 14

Relief flooded through Sam when he realized the troops on the road were Americans, not Mexicans. Against the advice of John, he had walked outside with the thought that, if he could convince the soldiers he was the only one here, maybe they would leave without causing any problems. When he saw that they were Americans, he called into the house and told everyone to come outside.

As the main convoy continued up the main road, a Hummer pulled out of line and roared up the two-track path towards the house. In a cloud of dust, it came to a stop next to Sam's truck. A door slammed and a ghostly form of a soldier slowly materialized out of the dust.

"What are you people doing here?" barked the soldier, stopping at the foot of the steps. "This area was supposed to have been evacuated yesterday."

"Stand at attention, soldier," demanded John, pushing Sam aside and stomping down the steps.

Sam blinked in surprise. John had become a totally different person.

The soldier looked John up and down. "Who the hell are you?" He stepped up and got right into John's face.

"Lieutenant Colonel John Redfeather," John shot back. "United States Army."

Sam watched the blood rush from the soldier's face.

As the soldier realized he was talking to a superior officer, he hastily stepped back and snapped to attention.

John took a step forward. "Now, *Captain*," he said, drawing out the word, "what's this about an evacuation?"

"Sir, yesterday we sent small contingents of troops throughout this area to inform all civilians to evacuate. As of this morning, this area was reported as being clear."

"Apparently, they missed this house," said Sam stepping next to John.

"At ease, soldier," John said.

The soldier relaxed and took a quick look over his shoulder at the procession of vehicles still passing by.

"What I want to know," said Sam, "is why these guys are here, behind enemy lines."

"Exactly what I was wondering." John looked intently at the soldier. "Captain, would you care to explain?"

He looked over his shoulder again. "All I can tell you is that this is part of the President's plan." He hastily added, "Sir."

The driver of the Hummer yelled out of the window, "Captain, we need to move out A.S.A.P. Scouts are reporting increased enemy movement. They think the Mexicans may be on to us."

"Shit," said the captain. He came to attention and saluted. "Sir, I'm sorry, but I need to continue my mission." He turned and ran to the Hummer. The driver made a u-turn and sped down the road.

"It's all part of the President's plan?" murmured John, rubbing his jaw and watching the Hummer as it merged into the line of vehicles slowly making their way up the road.

"What are you thinking?" Sam asked.

"I'm thinking that maybe the President isn't as stupid as I thought. Come on, let's go inside and I'll tell everybody what I think is going on. Then, we can decide what to do."

"Okay, but first you have to answer a question for me. Are you really a Lieutenant Colonel in the Army?"

John laughed. "No, not anymore, but he doesn't know

that." He looked at the retreating hummer.

* * *

Once inside, with everyone sitting in the living room, John said, "Okay, here's what I think is happening. I think the President pulled the troops away from all our southern bases on purpose to lure the Mexicans into attacking. Those soldiers weren't helping with the evacuation of the ash cloud. In reality, they were sent north, then secretly moved south, trying to cut off the Mexican troops.

Sam wasn't sure this was the intent of the President, but he didn't have a better thought to offer. He looked around at the confused faces of Lisa and Sunshine.

"Do you really think that's what happened?" asked Richard, a dubious look in his eyes.

"It's the only thing that makes sense. Why else would those troops be behind enemy lines?"

"Maybe they got trapped when the Mexicans moved north," Ashley said. "And they're trying to get back to our side."

John smiled at her. "I'm afraid not, sweetheart. A column that big wouldn't get bypassed easily."

Jean spoke up. "Well, regardless of why they're here, we still need to decide what we're going to do. Are we staying or are we going? Personally, I vote to stay."

"I vote we stay, too," said Lisa, pensively glancing around at everyone. "All in favor, raise your hand."

Everyone but Richard raised a hand.

"Well, I guess that settles it," said Jean, laying her hands in her lap. She turned to face Richard, waiting for his response.

Richard frowned as he looked at John and Sam. "I would like to know where those troops are going before we commit to anything. It's not that I don't believe you, John. I just want to make sure we're not making a big mistake by staying here."

"That's fine," John replied easily. "Sam and I can go out again and see where they're going and what they're doing."

Sam winced. The thought of the dead soldiers popped into his mind. He didn't think he could stomach the idea of picking up a weapon again so soon. "Um . . . why don't you take Richard this time," he suggested. "I don't think I'm up for another recon just yet, if you know what I mean."

Richard slapped his hands on his knees and stood up. "That's fine with me. It'll give me a chance to see the lay of the land while I'm out there."

Lisa stood up, too. "I wouldn't mind going. I think I need to get out for a while."

"Can I go this time?" Dave asked eagerly, his eyes begging Sam for a positive response.

Fear gripped Sam. His first instinct was to say no, but he realized Dave wasn't a little boy anymore. In six months. he would be eighteen and legally an adult. He needed to start making some decisions on his own . . . and Sam needed to start letting go. Sam looked to John and Richard to gage their responses.

They both shrugged their shoulders, indicating they didn't care one way or another.

Sam sighed and nodded to Dave. "Yes you can go, but I want you to listen to Richard and John. If they tell you to do something, do it, okay?"

"Yes, sir," he said enthusiastically, standing up and throwing Sam a poor imitation of a salute.

Sam caught Richard's eye and motioned towards the back patio. "Can I talk to you for a minute before you leave?"

"Sure," Richard said, ambling toward the back door.

Outside, Sam closed the door and spoke softly. "I have a favor to ask of you. I want you to watch Dave's reactions to whatever happens out there." From the confused look on Richard's face, Sam knew the man didn't understand what he was talking about. "I'm concerned that he's getting hooked on all this danger and excitement." He told Richard about Dave's reaction in Montrose when Sam had run away from the cop.

Richard said sympathetically, "Yes, I can see why you might be concerned. Addiction to excitement can be dangerous. Surviving the volcano, the mob in Casper where Linda had died, the ordeal in Montrose, and everything that's happened here, he might be starting to feel like he's invincible." He reached out and put his large hands on Sam's shoulders. "Don't worry, I'll watch him closely while we're out there. I'll let you know if I see anything you need to worry about."

Sam gave a sigh of relief. "Thanks, buddy, I owe you one."

"Actually, more than one," said Richard as he opened the door, "but who's counting?" He winked at Sam and walked into the house.

Is he talking about Linda? Sam wondered. *Or, is he talking about Lisa?*

* * *

While John, Richard, Lisa, and Dave were gone, Sam and Ashley pulled the camping equipment out of the truck and into the house. They sorted through the gear, deciding what to take down into the gun vault. Later, Sam helped Jean and Sunshine move all the non-perishable food from the kitchen to storage bins in the vault.

When Sam had done everything he could think of to

prepare for the upcoming stay at the house, he wandered around the rooms aimlessly, feeling useless, feeling depressed. When he couldn't stand pacing anymore, he called out to no one in particular, "I'm going for a walk. I've got some things I need to think about."

Sunshine yelled from the back bedroom, "That's fine. Just don't go too far, in case we need you."

"I won't," he answered as he exited the back door onto the deck.

Taking the same path he had taken with the kids two days earlier, he sat down on the same rock. He closed his eyes. Taking a deep breath and letting it out slowly, he concentrated on what was bothering him: Linda. He hadn't had a chance to properly mourn her death, and it seemed like now was the right time to put her memory to rest.

He lay back on the sun-warmed rock with his eyes closed and let the ghostly images of the past flash through his mind. He remembered the good times and the bad times that he and Linda had gone through. A single tear rolled down his cheek. Try as he might, he couldn't hold it in. The barriers around his emotions crumbled, leaving him curled up and sobbing his heart out for a love once pure and new, now dead and gone.

He lay on the rock until his emotions were spent.

Finally, sitting up, he dried his eyes. Taking a deep shuddering breath, he looked up at the sky. "Linda, wherever you are, I want you to know how sorry I am. Maybe if I would have spent less time working and more time with you, you wouldn't have felt the need to look for . . . for whatever it was you were looking for." He cleared his throat and wiped his eyes.

"And," he choked out, "I'm sorry for . . . getting you killed. I know I shouldn't blame myself, but I can't help but think that, if I hadn't taken that back road through

Casper that night, we wouldn't have run into that mob of crazy people, and you would still be here. Then, again, maybe it was meant to be." He took another deep breath, suppressing his emotions once again. "I love you, and you'll always have a place in my heart. Good bye, sweetheart."

The sound of a distant explosion brought him back to the problems of the present. "Shit." He jumped up, turned, and ran for the house.

Chapter 15

Out on the desert, Lisa held tightly to the overhead bar as John's Jeep hit a deep rut off the road and bounced. Her stomach lurched.

Dave sat next to her with a wild, excited look in his eyes.

"Now, what the hell's going on?" John growled as he brought the Jeep to an abrupt halt.

Lisa leaned forward, peering over Richard's shoulder to look out the windshield.

A convoy of army vehicles, coming over a low hill, headed straight towards them.

"It looks like the same vehicles that went past the house earlier," Lisa exclaimed. She swallowed hard. *This can't be good.*

"Yeah, it does," John responded, "except now, they seem to be in more of a hurry with less vehicles." John pulled the Jeep off the road to get out of the way.

As the convoy passed, a Hummer pulled out of line and made a beeline for them. It stopped next to the Jeep.

As it turned out, the same captain who had talked to them less than two hours earlier, leaned out his rolled-down window with a look of shock and disorientation. Dirt and blood spotted his uniform, now torn from multiple minor wounds. His hat was gone, and blood stained the side of his head. "Sir, I would advise you to return to your home, get your family, and follow us out of here while you can."

John nodded in the direction from where the army was retreating. "Why? What happened up there?"

"We were misinformed about the strength of the enemy," he said bluntly. "We got our asses kicked."

"Is the enemy following you?" Richard asked from the passenger's seat.

"Yes, but we're fighting as we pull back. We're trying to hold them off long enough to get our wounded out."

Suddenly, a loud explosion went off just a hundred yards away.

Lisa jumped with the others in the Jeep. She looked at a cloud of dust. "What the hell was that?"

"Artillery fire, Miss, from a 105-mm howitzer," said the captain, looking at her with concern on his face. "They have a range of just over two miles. That should tell you how close the enemy is."

John barked, "I understand, soldier, carry on."

The captain threw John a salute. "Take care, sir."

John nodded as the Hummer drove off. "Well, that changes things. Now, we have to leave and follow these guys out of here while we have the chance. Holing up in the shelter isn't a good option. We can only *hope* they won't find us there. It's a bigger risk."

Richard said calmly, "I agree."

Dave piped up with, "If we do stay at the house, we can make it look deserted. They'll probably take a quick look and just leave."

Richard eyed him and said, "We don't know how much time we'll have to make it look deserted. I think our best bet is to leave as soon as possible and follow these guys out."

John turned the Jeep around and slid into the convoy, which headed back towards the house. "Hold on," he said, suddenly turning off the main road, "I'm going to take a short cut. It's a little bumpier, but it will save us about ten minutes."

Lisa grabbed the roll bar as the vehicle headed up a

two-tired path weaving across the rocks and hard-packed dirt. Her heart raced at the hope they would make it back in time to pack and get out of the house.

Over the roar of the Jeep, Dave shouted, "The ash from the volcano is going to mess up their carburetors, so they won't be able to drive around very much anyway. All we have to do is survive tonight, and we should be okay, right?"

John blurted back, "I think so, but we don't know how much ash is going to fall and what kind of an impact it's going to have."

Lisa didn't like any of the options that seemed to loom in front of them. "So, on one hand, we need the ash to cripple the Mexicans' movements, and yet, on the other hand, it's going to cripple our army and us, too. It sounds like a no-win situation, no matter how you look at it."

"So, true," Richard said somberly. "But at least, we have somewhere to go to get out of the ash. They don't. Not only is it going to plug up their carburetors, it's going to get *inside* the vehicles and they're going to breathe it into their lungs. It's going to get in their food and water, so as they eat and drink, it will get into their stomachs. That ash is as fine as flour. There's no way they can keep it out. With any luck at all, it'll make them sick, maybe even kill some of them."

Dave, quietly looking out the back window, he turned around he said, "I know this is probably a stupid question, but I was looking at the dust behind us. Why would the ash affect the vehicles differently than this dust?"

"Well, with this kind of dust," John responded, "if you're the first vehicle in a line, there is no dust. If you're behind a vehicle, you can stay back far enough to stay out of it. With the ash, it doesn't matter where you are, you're going to be in it. Even when you're parked, it's going to fall and cover the vehicle."

"Okay," Dave said with a shrug, "that makes sense, I guess."

Richard looked over his shoulder at him. "And that's not all it will do. It's also going to get on their windshields. When they turn on their wipers, it's going to be like rubbing sandpaper on the glass. It's going to scour it so badly, they won't be able to see where they're going."

"So," asked Lisa, "if this ash is so abrasive, will it wear out their tires faster?"

Richard looked thoughtful for a minute. "I'm not sure, but I think so. It makes sense that it would."

Lisa sat forward to make her voice heard over the Jeep as it bounced over the rocks and headed directly toward the house. "I was just thinking ahead to when we leave. What kinds of problems will we be facing? How can we resolve them?"

"Smart thinking," said John as he parked in front of the house. "That is something we're going to have to deal with . . . eventually."

* * *

The afternoon sun felt warm as Lisa got out of the Jeep and hurried up the steps with the others. She looked behind her to see the American convoy just coming over the hill.

Sunshine opened the door before John reached it. Panic showed on her face. "Well, what did you find out? The fighting must be getting closer. We can hear the bombs going off from here." Her eyes fluttered from one person to the next for an answer.

"Why don't we get everybody together so I only have to tell it once," said John as he walked into the house.

"Well, in that case," Sunshine said, following him in, "we're going to have to wait a while until Sam gets back."

Lisa stopped short. "Why? Where did he go?"

"He went for a walk. He said he had some things he needed to think about."

Lisa's heart beat rapidly at the urgency to get on the road. Without entering the house, she turned and looked out over the desert. "Well, I hope he didn't go too far. We need to get out of here. How long has he been gone?"

"I don't know, a half-hour, forty-five minutes at the most," Sunshine answered from just inside the open door.

Richard scanned the horizon. "He couldn't have gone too far. Why don't Dave and I take a walk and see if we can find him?"

"Okay," Lisa said, taking charge, "you and Dave go find Sam. We'll start packing everything we can get into the vehicles." She hurried into the house to grab up her things.

A sudden, loud explosion out front rattled everything in the house.

John and Lisa ran back out the door. "Shit, it might be too late to leave now anyway. Look."

Lisa followed his pointed finger to the American troops by-passing the road heading up to the house. *Oh, no. That explosion means the Mexicans can't be far behind.* She turned to Richard, still standing on the porch. "*Go get Sam!*" she yelled.

He grabbed Dave's arm. "Yes, ma'am."

Sam appeared around the side of the house. Out of breath and panting, he rasped, "I heard the explosions. What's going on?"

"Let's go in the house and I'll explain," John said as he pushed his way past Ashley and Sunshine.

* * *

A short time later, after John had explained the situation, Lisa jumped up and started gathering up her personal things. She sensed the need to get out of there as soon as possible.

Jean looked at John and said, "There's no way we can leave. We took everything out of the vehicles and put it all in the shelter."

"We only have about five minutes," said Sam with a tone of urgency as he rose out of his chair. "We can only take what we can gather up in that time."

"I don't think we even have that long," said Ashley, standing at the front window.

Sam and John ran to the window.

Over their shoulder, Lisa could see the American army had almost disappeared out of sight. The Mexican's started coming down the road after them.

"Quick, everybody, get down to the vault," shouted John. "Only take weapons. Leave everything else."

Lisa dropped her backpack, grabbed her shotgun, and followed the others to the outside entrance of the vault. For a brief moment, she thought about the master-bedroom closet and wondered why they all took the long way through the back door to the storage shed. She lost the thought when she saw Sam peeking around the corner of the building.

He seemed to be standing watch as John opened the vault's door.

"Okay, everybody inside," John commanded.

Lisa carefully made her way to Sam. "Do you think they'll know we're here with the vehicles sitting there?"

"I don't know, maybe." He shrugged. "Hopefully, they'll think we left with the army and were in too much of a hurry to take them." Suddenly, he said, "I'll be right back."

Lisa watched him run to his truck. *What the hell is he doing?*.

He opened the front door and reached inside. Just as quickly, he ran to the other vehicles and performed the same action. When he returned, he held out his hand, showing her the keys. "I figured we shouldn't make it too easy for them to take our rides out of here. I'm sure, if they want to, they can hot-wire them, but hopefully, they won't want to take the time."

"Sam, Lisa," called John from down in the vault, "what the hell are you two doing? Get your asses down here."

Lisa stood at the bottom of the ladder as John closed the door, sealing them off from the outside world. She felt an overwhelming urge to yank John off the ladder and throw the door open. She closed her eyes and took a deep breath. *I'm not claustrophobic, so how come I'm feeling this way? Fear. I'm afraid. I'm afraid that whatever happens next isn't going to be good.*

Chapter 16

After five hours of being locked inside a vault with walls two-feet thick, making it impossible to hear anything outside, Sam was anxious to know what was happening above them. "What do you think?" he asked John. "Can we take a peek and see if there's anybody up there?"

John slipped the last 9mm round into the clip. He pushed it into the butt of the pistol until there was an audible click. "Do we need to?"

"I don't know." Sam shrugged. "I guess I'm just antsy. I can't stand being down here and not knowing what's going on up there." He pointed at the ceiling. "I keep imagining all kinds of horrible things."

"Like what?"

"Like there are thirty Mexican soldiers camped out in your living room, and when we open the door, they're going to swarm down here and take us prisoners or kill us."

John laughed. "So, we don't open the door."

"Doesn't it bother you . . . not knowing what's going on?"

"Not really. I figure whatever's going to happen is going to happen, and I'm not going to waste my time worrying about it." He got up and stretched. "In fact, I'm going to bed. In the morning, we'll open up and take a look."

Sam glanced around the vault as John and Sunshine headed for their two small cots in the corner. Dave and Ashley, quietly talking, both lay on the floor in sleeping bags. Richard and Jean, sitting in folding camp chairs, read books. Lisa sat at the table and wrote in a tablet.

"What are you writing?" Sam said, pulling out a chair and sitting down.

"I thought I would write down everything that has happened to me since the volcano blew up. You never know, maybe I can sell my story to a studio, and they will make it into the next big blockbuster movie." She chuckled.

"I guess you never know." He noticed her hands shaking. "Are you okay?"

Her face flushed. She self-consciously put her hands in her lap. "Yeah. I think I'm having a little bout of claustrophobia."

Sam grew instantly concerned. "How bad is it? You're not going to start running around, yelling, and bouncing your head off the walls, are you?"

Gripping the edge of the table, she caused it to shake. Her eyes got big. She started gasping. "I think I might. I feel like I'm going to lose it. I've got to get out of here. I can't breathe."

He stood up, knocking the chair back. "Damn, calm down, it's going to be . . . "

Lisa broke out laughing. "God, you are so gullible. You should see your face. You look like you're scared shitless."

"I am," he snarled. "The last thing we need is for someone to freak out down here."

"Hey, don't get your panties in a bunch." She giggled.

"Ha ha," said Sam, letting a smile break out on his face as he sat down again.

"By the way," she said, "I owe you an apology."

"What for?"

"If you remember right, when you said that to me I got a little bit upset."

"A little bit upset. I thought you were going to go get your shotgun and shoot me like you did Clem."

She laughed. "Actually, it's probably a good thing I didn't have it with me, or I might have. But seriously, I am sorry about the way I reacted. I think it was a combination of things that made me act that way."

"Like what?" he asked curiously.

"Well, I was upset because I had just lost everything I owned to Mother Nature. I was sad that I was alone, with nobody to lean on for help. I knew I would probably never be able to go home again. And, for some reason, when you made that comment, it made me think of Shawn."

"Aha. Now I think I understand. Panties are personal, and Shawn was the last person to . . . be personal with you, right?"

"Yeah, it felt like you were invading his territory or something." Staring at the table, she bit her lower lip. "I know he's gone and, sooner or later, I'll have to move on and start over with someone new, but I don't think I'm ready . . . yet." She looked at him. Her eyes conveyed the unspoken message.

"I know what you mean about not being ready . . . yet." He stared into her baby-blue eyes.

Lisa cleared her throat, breaking eye contact.

Sam sensed she was as nervous talking about this as he was.

"Oh, I just remembered. I have something else I want to ask you."

"Sure, ask away," he said, glad to move on to another subject.

"Our first morning here, you and I were sitting on the patio and talking. You started to tell me something about you and Linda, but you got interrupted when Dave came outside. What were you going to tell me?"

He thought back to the conversation, "Oh, yeah, I remember. I was about to tell you that, three days before the volcano blew, Linda and I had decided to file for divorce."

"That's kind of what I thought you were going to say. Do you mind if I ask why?"

Sam told her how he and Linda had drifted apart and that she was seeing someone else.

"I'm sorry to hear that. So, were you seeing someone?" she asked with raised eyebrows.

"No. I kept telling myself I didn't have the time or energy, but looking back now, I think the real reason I didn't get involved was because, at that time, I hadn't found anybody I liked."

"At that time?" She asked shyly, "Are you saying that now you've found somebody you like?"

"Let's just say that I'm thinking about a lot of things right now." He smiled and winked.

He wasn't sure where Lisa was going with this. Even though he liked her, he wasn't sure he wanted to get into this right now. Faking a yawn, he stretched. "I don't know about you, but I'm tired. I think I'm going to hit the hay."

She picked up her notebook, got up, and stood next to his chair. Reaching out, she gently brushed the backs of her fingers along his jaw. "Good night, Sam." She bent down and kissed him on the top of his head, then quickly walked away.

A flood of feelings washed over Sam as he turned and watched her head for her bed. Excitement, passion, and longing, mixed with guilt and sorrow, kept him sitting in the chair long after everyone else had fallen fast asleep.

* * *

The next morning, Sam woke up to the appetizing smell of fresh-brewed coffee. He rolled off his air mattress and, rubbing his back, stepped to the table,.

"What's wrong?" Richard asked. "You're walking like an old man."

"I must be getting old," Sam groaned. "I used to be able to sleep anywhere. Now, unless I sleep in a nice soft bed, I wake up feeling like somebody beat the shit out of me."

John set his coffee cup down. Smiling at Sam, he leaned back on his chair. "Do you think your old decrepit body can make it upstairs to see what's going on?"

"If you'll give me five minutes to drink a cup of coffee," Sam shot back, "I'll race you up the ladder." Sam eagerly took the cup of coffee Sunshine offered him.

"Richard," Lisa said, chuckling as she approached, "maybe you'd better follow him up so that if he falls, you can catch him."

"Ha, ha," Sam said, turning to look at her. "I see you're limping a little bit this morning, too. What's wrong, are you getting old, too?"

She cuffed him playfully on the head. "No, I slept wrong, that's all."

Richard stood up. "Okay, you two, that's enough talk about being old. You're reminding me that Jean and I are the oldest ones here."

Sunshine pushed a stray strand of hair out of her face. "You may be the oldest of the group, but I'll bet you're in better shape than any of us."

"Okay, enough chit-chat," said John, "Are you ready Sam?"

"Yeah, let's go take a look and see what's going on topside. Who else is going?" Sam looked around the group.

"Can I go?" Dave jumped up off of his sleeping bag.

"Please, please, please," he begged, pressing his palms together as if he was praying.

"I know you're not claustrophobic," said Sam, "so why do you want to get out of here so bad?"

"I want to see if any ash fell last night, and I'm curious to see if anybody came looking for us." He was so excited, he almost bounced from one foot to the other.

Sam stared hard at him for a moment. *He looks like a junkie in need of a fix.* "Okay, I guess you can go with us," he reluctantly replied.

"I'd like to go up," Ashley said.

"We want to go, too," Richard said, putting his arm around Jean.

"Me, too," called out Sunshine.

Lisa said, "Apparently, I'm not the only one that needs to get out of here for a little while."

Sam smiled at her wryly. "Well, you can't blame them, being cooped up in here is like being in prison or trapped in a cave. It's just plain no fun. Okay, everybody let's go see what's going on up there." He looked to John to take the lead.

"Wait a minute," John said abruptly, "aren't you forgetting something?"

"I don't think so." Sam glanced around.

"Do you think you should take your gun? What if there are thirty Mexican soldiers sitting in my living room waiting for you?"

Suddenly, Sam's fears from the previous night returned. "You're right," he said. "We all need to take our guns with us."

"Do you really think there're soldiers up there?" Ashley whispered, her eyes wide with fear.

"No, sweetheart, I don't," Sam said, putting his arm around her. "But it wouldn't hurt to be prepared."

With the exception of Sunshine and Jean, the others

strapped guns to their waists.

"Okay," Sam stated firmly, "it looks like we're ready. Let's go." He followed John towards the ladder that opened into the master bedroom closet.

At the ladder, John paused. "Let me go up first and make sure it's safe." He climbed up, punched in the code, then slowly lifted the door just far enough to scan the room.

"What can you see?" whispered Sam.

"The inside of the closet door," John snapped back. "Be quiet. I'll be right back." He opened the door all the way and slipped out of sight.

Sam nervously waited for what seemed like an eternity. Then, he heard, "Pssst." He looked up.

John waved to him.

As Sam climbed the ladder and entered the closet, John quietly said, "As far as I can tell, there's nobody around. Go ahead and go into the living room. I'll send everybody else in."

* * *

With his hand on the butt of his pistol, Sam swallowed hard and walked cautiously through the kitchen. Half-expecting Mexican soldiers to jump out and shoot him at any moment, he stopped at the entrance to the living room and held his breath. His eyes darted nervously around the room until he was satisfied no one was there. Walking slowly to the window next to the front door, he separated the mini blinds and peeked out into a cloudy desert. "Would ya look at that?" he muttered. A grayish powder, looking like snow, covered everything in sight. *It's ash from the volcano.*

"What's out there?" someone said right behind him.

"Son of a bitch," he yelled as he spun around and

yanked out his gun.

"Wow, Sam," Lisa said, holding up her hands. "Take it easy. It's just me."

His hands shook so badly, he had to use both of them to get his gun back into the holster. "Jesus, woman, don't sneak up on me like that. You scared the piss out of me."

Lisa giggled. "Did you think I was a Mexican soldier here to kill you?"

"As a matter of fact, I did," he snapped.

"It's a good thing I'm not. Your hands are shaking so badly, I don't think you could hit the broad side of a barn." She giggled again.

Now that he was over the first flush of fear, he started to see the humor in the situation. "You're right. Well, I never claimed to be another Rambo." He chuckled and shrugged his shoulders.

"You never did answer me," Lisa insisted. "What's out there?"

"Take a look for yourself." He moved out of her way.

"Wow, is that ash? It looks like dirty snow."

"I wish it was snow," he remarked. "It would be a lot easier to deal with." Still jumpy and concerned for the others, he looked around to find them all looking out windows.

"How much do you think is out there?" Lisa asked.

He rubbed his jaw and tried to estimate from the layer on the Jeep. "I don't know for sure, but if I had to guess, I'd say an inch . . . two at the most."

John approached. "I don't see any tracks, so I don't think anybody's been here, at least not since it stopped falling."

Lisa glanced back out the window. "You're right. I didn't notice, but it isn't falling anymore."

Richard turned on the T.V. "I'll see if I can find out what's going on in the world."

Ashley, looking a little pale and haggard, stepped next to John. "If nobody's been here, why did we have to stay down in the vault? Couldn't we have stayed up here?"

Sam shot John a look. "Um, I guess we could have," Sam mumbled.

"You're right," John agreed, "we could have. But I didn't want to take the chance that whoever was on watch would fall asleep and that we would get taken by surprise if somebody showed up."

"You know," Ashley responded, "you need to learn to trust people more." She flipped back her long blond hair as she turned and walked away.

Overhearing this, Sunshine laughed. "See, honey, I keep telling you, but you won't listen to me. Maybe hearing it from someone else, you'll realize it's true."

"Yeah, I know," he replied, giving Sam a sheepish look, "but I never have been the trusting type."

"*Yes!*" Richard yelled from his seat in front of the T.V.

Sam hurried to his side. "What's happening?"

"The jet stream has changed direction. It's pushing the ash cloud east again. And, there's a storm system moving into this area later today that's supposed to bring rain with it."

"Is that a good thing?" inquired Jean, standing behind Sam.

Richard shifted in his seat. "Yeah . . . think about it. The rain's going to soak the ash and turn it into mud. Then, as it dries out, it will be . . . ."

"*Dried* mud," blurted Dave from the window.

"That's right. The rain will bond it together so it won't be as apt to fly up and be a problem."

"How long is the storm going to last?" asked Sam.

"Just today," Richard responded. "Hopefully, we can leave by tomorrow morning."

Ashley groaned. "Do we have to spend another night

downstairs in that vault? I don't like it down there."

All eyes locked on John.

John looked around the room. "I think we'll be okay to stay up here tonight. I don't think the Mexicans will be moving their troops around too much with all this ash on the ground. But, I do want to keep someone on watch at all times."

"Okay, then," said Sam, seeing a sense of relief coming over Ashley and feeling less pensive about the immediate danger, "I guess that settles it."

John stepped forward. "Before it rains, we need to go out and sweep the ash off the vehicles. If that stuff gets wet and dries, we'll never get it off."

"I'll grab you guys a couple of brooms," said Sunshine, scurrying to the kitchen.

"Come on, Dave," Richard said, rising out the chair, "you can help us."

"While you do that," Jean called out as she started into the kitchen, "us women will start fixing breakfast."

Sam hadn't thought about food until now, but he suddenly realized how good breakfast sounded. He hoped it would be ready by the time they finished sweeping the vehicles.

* * *

Outside, little clouds of dust puffed up with every step Sam took.

"Make sure you don't breath any of this ash," Richard advised.

John started down the steps. "I have some dust masks in the storage shed out back. I'll be right back."

When he returned, Sam donned his mask and proceeded with John, Richard, and Dave to clear the ash off all three vehicles.

They finished just as a bolt of lightning flashed across the sky. Almost as though the lightning signaled the storm to start, the wind started blowing, picking up the ash and swirling it around.

"Well, a lot of good that did," Sam moaned, watching the ash settled on the vehicles again.

Richard called out in warning, "Come on, let's get in the house before we end up covered in this shit."

"I agree," said Sam growing nervous. As he turned and headed for the house, a large explosion went off on the other side of the vehicles.

Dazed, Sam suddenly realized he was lying on the ground. His ears rang. Sitting up, he looked around. Richard and Dave lay on the ground, too. Only John moved. Sam could barely hear John yelling, "Hurry and get into the house."

"What the hell was that?" Sam shouted. "Lightning?"

"No, it was an artillery shell," John shouted back, helping Sam get to his feet and shoving him towards the house. "Now, get your ass up and in the house."

Sam stumbled over to Dave, who was lying on his stomach. Gently rolling him over, Sam felt queasy at the sight of a four-inch gash across Dave's forehead, just below his hair line. "Dave's hurt," he called to John, who was leaning over Richard.

"Pick him up and get him in the house," yelled John, "or he might end up dead."

Sam picked up Dave in a fireman's carry and stumbled towards the house.

Lisa stood at the open door and waved him in.

Laying Dave down on the floor in the living room, Sam returned to check on John and Richard.

John struggled to lift Richard's two-hundred-and-eighty-pound body off the ground.

"Shit!" Sam exclaimed as he ran to help John. .

"I told you to get in the house," John barked.

"I can't leave you and Richard out here. There's no way you can get him inside by yourself, so shut up and let's get him inside."

They each grabbed an arm, slinging him over their shoulders. Richard's feet left twin furrows in the ash as they struggled to drag him up the steps and into the house.

Lisa met them at the door.

Jean, with worry etched on her forehead, slammed the door shut as soon as they got Richard inside.

"Quick, everybody down to the vault," cried John as he and Sam dragged Richard across the carpet and headed for the ladder in the closet.

Sam looked over his shoulder to see if Dave was awake. Seeing no movement, he feared that Dave's injury might be serious. He also feared he wouldn't have time to come back and get Dave into the vault before it was too late.

"Don't worry about Dave, Sam," Jean said, catching his eye. "We'll bring him with us."

"Okay, but hurry." Sam felt a sense of panic overtaking him at the thought of the soldiers growing closer and the vault seeming like a million miles away. Would they all make it to safety?

By the time John and Sam reached the closet, Richard started to come around. They gently laid him down next to the shaft.

Sam slapped Richard hard on the cheek.

"What the hell are you doing?" asked John with a frown.

"Trying to bring him around."

"You don't have to slap him so hard."

Richard shook his head and blinked his eyes. "Yeah, you about knocked me out again."

"Sorry," Sam said uncomfortably. "I've never had to do anything like this before. I'm just doing what I've seen people do in movies."

John shot Sam an exasperated look and shook his head. "Richard, do you think you can climb down the ladder on your own?"

"I think so. As long as Sam doesn't slap me anymore." He looked at Sam expectantly.

"Hey," Sam blurted, "I said I was sorry."

"Don't worry about it," said Richard. He sat up and patted Sam on the cheek. "I forgive you."

"What the hell are the three of you doing?" Lisa demanded as she entered the closet. "I thought you would be down the ladder already."

"Hey," John barked, "I don't know about you, but I would rather have Richard climb down on his own. I don't think I can carry him down on my back."

"Whatever," she muttered and turned away.

Richard started down the ladder as Sunshine and Ashley arrived with Dave suspended between them. Richard paused just before his head went below the rim. "Where's Jean?" he asked, trying to see around them.

"She'll be here in a minute," Sunshine answered. "She's making sure the stove's off and gathering up breakfast. We worked hard making it, and we didn't want it to go to waste."

He eagerly nodded his head. "Good, I'm hungry." He ducked down out of sight.

Sunshine rolled her eyes. "Men . . . you're all the same."

Sam knelt next to Dave. "Is he still out?" he asked Ashley, who seemed surprisingly calm, considering the circumstances.

"Yeah, he is, but how are we going to get him down there?"

"We'll set him on the side of the opening," John said, "and hold him by the arms. Then, we can lower him down to Richard."

Sam nodded. He picked up Dave's shoulders while John picked up his feet. They set him on the edge of the shaft. Sam glanced down at Richard. "Are you sure you can handle him?"

"I don't know. Maybe you need to come down and slap me first," he said sarcastically, "to make sure I'm awake."

John chuckled and eyed Sam. "I don't think you're ever going to live that down."

"Ha ha," Sam shot back. "Just help me lower him, will ya?"

After they lowered Dave, Sam turned to see Jean arrive. He motioned for the women to go first and stepped out of their way as they passed by, one by one.

"You're next," said John as another explosion rocked the trailer house.

"No problem. I don't mind going next." Sam scrambled down the ladder with John right behind him.

John shut and locked the door.

Sam said, "So, is this place strong enough to stand a direct hit by one of those artillery shells?"

"Yes. Remember, this place has walls two-feet thick." John climbed down the ladder. "Don't worry about it. Right now, you need to worry about Dave."

"You're right," said Sam, heading towards the cot where Dave had been laid. "How is he?" he asked Richard.

"He'll be fine. As far as I can tell, he doesn't have a concussion, but I won't know for sure until he wakes up."

"Are you going to stitch up that gash on his forehead?"

"Not until he wakes up. I don't want to be in the

middle of it and have him start thrashing around."

Suddenly, Dave moaned and tossed his head from side to side.

Jean turned from setting the food on the table. "I'll get the suture kit. It looks like he's waking up now."

As soon as Dave opened his eyes, Sam said, "Hi, son. How are you feeling?"

"Lousy. I feel like somebody hit me in the head with a baseball bat. What happened?" He started to get up.

Sam gently pushed him back down. "An artillery shell hit next to the truck and knocked us all down. You and Richard seemed to have taken a more direct hit."

"Are you okay, Richard?" Dave asked the big man.

"Yeah, I just got a little bump to the head, but you, on the other hand, need some stitches. So, just lay there and relax. Jean and I will fix you up as good as new."

Sam felt the ground vibrate under his feet. A lump came to his throat. He raised his eyebrows to John, who was eating a bowl of cereal at the table. "Are you sure this place . . . ?"

"Yes, Sam," John cut in, "this place can handle it. I promise."

As the ground shook again, Sam didn't feel convinced by John's confidence. His stomach wrenched. He had lost his appetite. He decided to leave Dave in the capable hands of Richard and Jean and check on Ashley, who was leaning against the wall with her arms folded. "How about you, Ash? Are you doing okay?"

"I'm fine, Dad. I think I'm getting used to everything that's been happening to us. It isn't bothering me like it used to. Sunshine told me the easiest way to deal with all this stuff is to ignore it, not think about it all the time. It seems to be working."

"That's great, honey." A sudden wave of dizziness passed over him. "I think I'm going to lay down for a minute, okay?"

"Sure, Dad."

Lying down on his sleeping bag, he closed his eyes and wondered how he was going to get through all of this. *Sunshine gave Ashley some good advice. Maybe I need to stop thinking about everything so much.*

* * *

Lisa sat at the table across from John and sipped a cup of coffee. She shivered each time the ground shook. She didn't see how John could be so cool and detached about the situation when the Mexican soldiers were obviously attacking close by.

When John finished his cereal and got up from the table, Ashley sat down in his place.

"Do you mind if I ask you something?" she asked quietly.

Lisa smiled. "No, you can ask me anything you want." *She is really a beautiful young lady with her long, silky hair and green eyes. I wonder if she looks like her mother.*

"Do you love my dad?"

Shocked at the bluntness of the question, Lisa took a moment to think about what she wanted to say and how she wanted to say it. Finally, she said, "If you're looking for a simple 'yes' or 'no,' I'm afraid I can't answer your question. It's a little more complicated than that."

Ashley sat back and folded her arms. "Why?"

Lisa sighed. "Because I lost my husband six months ago, and your dad lost his wife . . . your mother . . . less than a week ago. There's also you and Dave to consider."

"I didn't know about your husband." Ashley paused as Lisa took another sip of coffee. "And I'm sorry he died. But I want you to know that you don't need to worry about me and Dave. If you and my dad want to get married, we won't stand in your way."

Lisa choked, spitting coffee across the table. "Married?" she blurted. "What makes you think we want to get married?"

"See," Ashley said, flashing Lisa an innocent smile, "Dave and I aren't the only ones who are concerned about how fast this thing between the two of you is going."

Lisa had to give Ashley credit. She had set her up perfectly. She returned the smile. "It's not moving that fast. I admit there are some feelings, but that's all it is right now . . . just feelings."

"Maybe so," Ashley said with a shrug, "but I just want the two of you to take it slow, for the sake of everybody involved. There's a lot at stake for all of us, and I wouldn't want you to jump into something and then regret it later."

"You mean me stepping into your mother's place."

"No, nobody can ever replace my mom." Ashley's green eyes turned hard and dark.

Lisa leaned forward, resting her arms on the table. She looked directly at Ashley. "If, and I mean *if*, your dad and I get serious, I promise I will never try to replace her. I would much rather be your friend than your stepmom."

Ashley slowly nodded her head. "Okay, I just needed to know where you were coming from." The hardness faded. Her eyes sparkled again. "By the way, I meant what I said about me and Dave not standing in your way. We talked about it the other night and decided that Mom and Dad were going to get a divorce anyway. Sooner or later, he would have met somebody. We can see that he likes you and, well, we like you, too. We just aren't ready for a new mom, yet."

Lisa was touched by the sincerity in Ashley's voice.

"Thank you, Ashley, for letting me know how you and Dave feel about this whole thing. To tell you the truth, this is a relief. I was wondering how I could talk to you about the situation without causing a problem. I'm so glad you came to me first. Oh, by the way, I never did answer your question. I'm not sure about love, but I do *like* your dad. A lot."

They stood up and hugged.

This is one smart girl, Lisa thought. *I hope I can live up to her expectations.*

* * *

Sam watched Ashley get up and give Lisa a hug. *That's different. I wonder what they were talking about. I'm sure I heard Lisa say something that sounded like "married." Why would they talk about marriage? And why would Lisa choke and spit coffee across the table when she said it?*

"Sam," Richard called, interrupting his thoughts, "could you come over here for a minute?"

"Yeah, I'll be right there." He swung his feet to the floor and got up.

Dave was now sitting on the cot. A neat row of stitches ran across his forehead, about an inch below his hairline.

"I guess I won't be able to complain about you growing your hair out now," Sam said. "You'll have to hide that scar."

"Actually, it shouldn't leave much of a scar," said Richard, packing up his medical kit. "I'm thinking it was a piece of glass or something similar that hit him. Whatever it was, it made a nice clean cut. I was able to stitch it closed using the smallest suture I had."

"How are you feeling?" Sam put his hand on Dave's

shoulder. "Does it hurt?"

"No, not too bad," he said a little groggily. "Jean gave me a shot of something."

"And now, you need to sleep," said Jean, gently easing him down on the cot. "You can talk to him later." She shooed Sam and Richard away with a wave of her hand.

As they moved to the opposite side of the room, Sam said, "So, what about you? Are you okay?"

Richard rubbed the back of his head. "Yeah, it takes more than a bump on the head to stop me," he chuckled. "By the way, thanks for coming back and helping John get me inside. Jean told me about it."

Sam reached out and put his hand on Richard's shoulder. "Hey, no problem. I owe you. And do you really think I could stand there and not help a friend in need?"

"Thanks again, my friend." Richard stuck out his hand.

Sam took it in his and looked into Richard's grateful eyes. "You're welcome, friend."

Chapter 17

The next morning, as Sam poured himself a cup of coffee, John came down the ladder. "Well," Sam asked, "how does it look up there?"

"Good. I went outside and it looks like it's going to be a beautiful day. There's not a cloud in the sky, and the ash is already drying. Also, I checked the vehicles for damage from the artillery shell. We were lucky. Other than some minor dings and dents, there's nothing wrong with them."

"Great, that's good news. I worried about that all night. Now, maybe we can get out of here and, with any luck at all, we won't have any more problems." Sam took a deep breath, slowly releasing it as he looked around the room at the others, all gathered together for the next leg of their unpredictable journey.

"I didn't know we we're going to leave," John said.

"Well, we obviously can't stay here," Richard retorted as he stood next to Jean. "It's far too dangerous."

"That's true," Lisa said. "What happened yesterday proved that."

Ashley and Dave nodded in agreement.

"I think we should head for Oregon and my brother's place," Sam said, hoping John would agree and they could get out of there before they got attacked again.

John hesitated.

Sam could see the indecision on his face.

"Okay, we'll go," John finally said. "But you do realize we can't go north because of the ash? We're going to have to go west to Barstow, then cut north."

"That's okay," Sam said. "As long as we're leaving, I don't care which way we go."

"We'll need to take a drive and see if the Mexican army's still blocking our path," John said, looking intently at Sam.

A good night's sleep and the promise of getting away from here to someplace safe had Sam raring to go. "Not a problem," he said. "I'll even go with you."

"It's settled then," Jean said nervously. "Let's get packed and go while we can."

Everybody scattered to gather their things while John and Sam drove to the hill where they had been the day before. They returned with good news. The Mexican army was nowhere in sight, giving the group a clear shot to I-40 and Barstow.

"It's a real shame you've got to leave this place behind," Sam said as he helped John pack up guns and ammo.

"Well," remarked John casually, "it's not like I'm going to be gone forever."

Sam's eyes widened in surprise. "You mean you're coming back?"

"Of course. Why wouldn't I?"

"I don't know." Sam shrugged. "I just assumed you and Sunshine would stay with us in Oregon."

"No way. It's not that we don't like you guys, and I'm sure Oregon's nice, but we like it here. This is our home. Once the Mexicans are gone, there's no reason not to come back."

Sam nodded his head in agreement but felt a pang of disappointment. "You're right."

"Hey, don't look so sad. You can come visit us whenever you want. And, on the plus side, if you ever need to run away from a killer volcano, you'll have someplace to go." John slapped Sam on the shoulder.

"Come on, let's get these up to the truck and get something to eat."

By the time they finished a quick breakfast and loaded their supplies into the vehicles, the sun had warmed and dried the ash, just as Richard had predicted. The rain had washed most of the ash off the vehicles.

* * *

On the road toward the highway, Sam saw a few tire tracks, but no other signs of humans. This gave him a sense of relief, although he knew he would have to remain on the alert. He looked at Lisa. She sat silently with her arm resting over the open window. Through the rearview mirror, he observed Ashley holding a pillow against her chest as she stared blankly out the window. Dave's head rested against the back of the seat with his eyes closed. The gash on his head seemed red and sore, but already healing. Sam swallowed hard, hoping they would all get through this unscathed.

When they arrived at I-40, John stopped in an open desert area and had everyone gather around his Jeep. He cleared his throat. "Okay, listen up. If the vehicle in front of you starts making dust, make sure you stay back far enough to keep out of it. We don't want any plugged carburetors. Also, keep your phones handy. If I run into trouble, I'll call you." He pointed at Sam. "Sunshine will call Richard and Jean."

"Okay," said Sam. "Why don't you lead, since you know where we're going? I'll bring up the rear." Suddenly, Sam's cell phone rang. "Who in the hell could that be ? Hello?"

"I just wanted to see if the network was still working," said Richard's deep voice.

Sam gave the big man a quick glance and hung up.

"Apparently, it is."

Richard turned to John. "Give us your number, John, in case we have to call you."

"That's a good idea."

They all exchanged numbers, putting them into their phones.

"Okay, let's head out," barked John. "Next stop, Barstow, California."

* * *

Ten miles later, as Sam caught sight of the bridge crossing the Colorado River from Arizona to California, John and Richard slammed on their brakes. Sam hit his brakes, too, bringing gasps from Lisa and Ashley.

Dave lurched forward and grabbed the back of Sam's seat.

As Sam came to a halt, he saw a Mexican army Jeep and a tank, sitting in the middle of the freeway and completely blocking the bridge. His heart jumped into his throat. Although Lisa and the kids remained silent, Sam could feel their tension.

John spun his Jeep around and sped back towards Sam. Richard followed closely behind.

With his hands shaking, Sam quickly turned his vehicle around to keep up. He followed them to a nearby exit, taking a winding two-lane road that edged an aquatic wildlife reserve. Sam looked in the mirrors to see if they were being chased, but his truck kicked up so much dust, he couldn't see anything behind him.

After five miles on the winding road, they climbed a small hill and came to a junction.

Sam saw an old gas station on one side of the road and a bar on the other side.

John pulled over at the gas station.

As Sam pulled in behind him, he noticed signs on the pumps: *No gas available.* He looked at his gas gage. *It's a good thing our tanks are pretty much full.* As he got out of the truck, he looked at Lisa and the kids. "Unless you need to use the bathroom, stay in the truck. I don't think we'll be here very long."

Lisa nodded silently and the kids fell back into their seats in compliance.

Sam wondered about Lisa, who seemed to be so quiet since they had gotten up. *Is she frightened, or is she pondering what she and Ashley had been discussing the previous day.*

John unfolded a map and laid it out on the hood of his Jeep. "This is where we are now," he said to Richard and Sam. "If we take this road north, we'll end up here, in Bullhead City. We can cross the river from there into Laughlin, Nevada, head to Searchlight, then west to I-15."

"You can't go that way," a voice said behind them.

Startled, all three spun around.

"The bridge is gone." The young man, probably in his early twenties, Sam guessed, stared at them with his piercing brown eyes. He wore the latest punk-style outfit, complete with shaved head and pierced lips and ears.

John recovered first. "What about the road over Davis Dam? Is that still passable?"

"Nope, the army's got it blocked. They're afraid someone will try to blow it up."

"Do they have the bridge that crosses at the Avi Casino closed, too?"

"Yup," the guy answered, the jewel in his lip catching a ray of the sun. "As far as I know, the only road they're letting anyone use is Highway 68 to Kingman."

"And," drawled John, "I suppose from there, they're sending everybody to Vegas."

"Nope. They're making everybody stay in Kingman. They won't let anybody go across the new Hoover Dam Bridge, either."

"We came through Kingman on our way down from the north," interjected Richard. "Isn't that quite a ways east of here?"

"Yeah," John stated flatly, "and you're not going back there, if I have anything to say about it." He seemed staunchly determined to get them to California, one way or another. "What about Parker Dam or the bridge that crosses the river at Parker. Can we get across there?"

"That's too far south of here for me to know anything about," said the young man. "Besides, that whole area is behind enemy lines. You'd be crazy to go that way."

"Yeah, you're right," responded John, "but there's got to be some way to get across the river. There's no way I'm going to go to Kingman and sit there forever."

"Whatever," said the man as he turned and sauntered away.

Sam's throat felt dry. He wondered if they should just go back to the house and wait it out in the vault. None of the options sounded friendly or safe.

"So, what are we going to do now?" asked Richard.

"We're going to see if we can cross at the casino bridge. That's on an Indian reservation. Maybe we'll get lucky and they'll let us cross." John shrugged his shoulders.

When Sam got inside the truck, he explained the situation to Lisa, Dave, and Ashley. "So, when we get there, I want all of you to be quiet and try to look desperate. Maybe it will help in them allowing us to cross."

* * *

Sam followed Richard and John until they came to the bridge. When they stopped, Sam could see only one Hummer, parked sideways, on the opposite end. "Well, this doesn't look too bad."

Lisa nodded. "You're right, it doesn't look that bad. I wonder why they only have one vehicle guarding this bridge."

"Who knows?" Sam shrugged his shoulders. "Like God, sometimes the army works in mysterious ways." As Sam drove past the Hummer, one of the three bored-looking soldiers waved, then went back to playing cards.

After they had passed the casino, John pulled over, got out, and laid a map out on the hood of his Jeep. As Richard and Sam approached, he said, "Okay, now that we're across the river, we have two choices. We can go south and catch the freeway again and continue heading west, or we can head north to Searchlight and Vegas, then up Highway 95 to Reno and on into Oregon. " He traced the two options with his finger.

Without looking at the map, Richard said, "I vote we head back to the freeway and keep heading west. The farther north we go, the thicker the ash is going to be and we don't know what the situation is like in Vegas. It could be bad."

"I agree," said Sam, thinking about the hassle of going back through the same potential problems they had faced when heading south. "We'd be better off going west."

"Okay then, let's go," said John as he folded the map.

* * *

Sam didn't see another car for two hours. The ash faded with the miles, and the world seemed almost normal once again. About five miles before they reached Ludlow, Sam's phone rang. He handed it to Lisa.

"Answer it, and put it on the speaker so we can all hear ."

After punching a few buttons. Lisa said, "Hello."

"Hi, Lisa, it's John. Richard's on the line, too. This is a three-way call so that you can all hear what I have to say."

Sam instantly picked up on the seriousness in John's voice. He sat up straighter in his seat and began to feel old stomach wrenching at the new problems they might have to face.

"Go ahead, John, we're listening," Lisa said as she stared intently at the phone.

Dave and Ashley leaned their arms against the back of the seats so they could hear better.

Sam noticed the tension in their faces, not expecting good news.

"You may not be able to see it from where you are, but a Mexican army Jeep is on the other side of the freeway . . . the east bound side. I don't know if he's going to parallel us, or if he's going to try to cross over and get behind us."

Sam looked ahead at the eastbound lanes. He caught sight of the jeep as it came up onto the freeway from the shoulder and picked up speed. "So, what are we going to do?" Sam asked, as he looked around and wondered if there were other jeeps in the area.

"We're going to take the next exit and head out into the desert. Maybe we can lose him out there."

"And if we can't lose him?" asked Richard.

"Then we'll deal with him out there," John coldly replied, leaving no doubt as to what he meant.

Sam heard faint popping noises coming over the phone.

"*Oh, shit*, he's shooting at us," John yelled.

"What can we do to help you?" Richard asked in an anxious tone.

"Nothing, just follow me as fast as you can go."

As they approached the next exit, Sam looked at the Jeep to his left and then to the stop sign at the end of the exit. "I hope there's no cop around, because I'm not about to stop." He blew past the stop sign with a hard right turn and headed north into the desert. Looking in his rearview mirror, he saw the Jeep was now only about two hundred yards behind him. A Dairy Queen restaurant flashed by on his right, then he was on a dirt road with nothing around him but flat desert.

"Oh shit, this is not good," he called out as a bullet shattered his driver's-side mirror, leaving a perfectly round hole in the plastic housing. He could see nothing ahead of him because of the dust kicked up by John and Richard. He turned the wheel slightly to the left and swerved out onto the desert.

"What are you doing?" shouted Lisa. "You're not on the road anymore."

"What road?" he shot back. "There is no road. It's just two-tire tracks in the dirt."

Once out of the dust, he saw that Richard had done the same thing, only to the right side of the road. Seeing nothing in his way, Sam floored the gas pedal. The big V-8 jumped to life, sending the truck flying across the hard-packed dirt. He watched as the speedometer went to fifty, to sixty, to seventy, then he hit a dip and went airborne.

"*Oh, shit!*" he yelled as the truck flew through the air. When it landed, it hit so hard, Sam lost his grip on the steering wheel. The wheel spun to the left, throwing the truck into a slide. Sam slammed on the brakes and grabbed the steering wheel, fighting to keep the truck from flipping over as it slid sideways. He brought it to a stop in a huge cloud of dust.

Letting out his breath in relief, he looked at his passengers. "Is everybody okay?" He wiped the sweat from his forehead with the back of his hand.

"Yeah, I think so," said Dave.

"I'm fine," Ashley whispered.

"I'm okay, no thanks to you." Lisa complained. "What the hell were you thinking driving that fast. I . . . "

"I was trying to get away from *him*," Sam shouted as he pointed to the army Jeep pulling up in front of them.

"Oh, oh," Lisa half-whispered, her eyes widening with fear.

"*Oh, oh*, is right," Sam said, looking down the barrel of the fifty-caliber machinegun mounted on the roof of the Jeep. He couldn't help but notice that the gunner was pointing it straight at him.

His phone rang. Afraid to move, he decided not to answer it.

The gunner lifted his left hand and moved his fingers in the universal sign of goodbye, then placed his hand back on the gun.

Sam expected to see flames shoot out of the barrel and to feel the bullets tear into his body.

Suddenly, as if by magic, the Jeep exploded.

Lisa and Ashley both let out ear-piercing screams as pieces of the Jeep and bodies flew into the air.

Sam instinctively ducked as a loud roar filled the cab. He watched in amazement as an F-16 Fighter Jet buzzed over the truck.

The pilot made a long, slow turn. As he came back across the front of the truck, he turned the plane on its side. He flew low enough for Sam to see him wave and give a thumbs-up sign. The pilot, then, lit it up and disappeared over the mountains with the roar of the afterburner still shaking the truck.

Sam's phone rang again. He grabbed it and hit the talk button. "What?"

"I'm glad you finally answered," John bellowed. "Are

you guys all right?"

"Yeah, we're fine . . . I think." He quickly scanned his passengers. "Just a little shaken up."

"Okay, that's a relief," John confessed. "We're stopped about a half a mile up the road. Why don't you come up here and we'll decide what to do now?"

Sam hung up, placed his hands on the wheel, and leaned his forehead against them for a moment to gather himself together. He looked up into his rearview mirror.

Dave no longer looked excited by all the action. In fact, it looked to Sam as though he was scared as hell. *Good, maybe that knock on the head knocked some sense into him.*

* * *

When Sam pulled up to the others, John, Sunshine, Richard, and Jean were standing outside their vehicles. "That was a little intense," said Sam as he got out of the truck and approached them.

"I'll bet," said Sunshine, looking haggard with dust in her hair and a serious concern in her eyes. "It looked pretty intense from here, too." She met Ashley with a hug.

Jean said somberly, "We couldn't tell if it was you or the Mexicans that blew up. We're so glad you made it."

Sam shook his head. "If it hadn't been for that jet coming out of nowhere and taking out that Jeep, it *would* have been us. The guy in the Jeep had that fifty-caliber machinegun pointed right at us, and I'm positive he was about to open fire."

"Well, if you're sure everybody's okay," John said, turning to get in his Jeep, "we need to get out of here before someone sends one of the other Jeeps to see what happened to these guys."

Lisa stepped forward nervously. "What other Jeeps? Were there others back there?"

"There were at least two more Jeep's and a tank sitting at the exit," Richard said. "Didn't you see them?"

Sam shook his head. "No, and it doesn't matter now." He called after John. "So what now? If there are more of them behind us, we can't go back. Is there another way out of here?"

"According to my GPS, about five miles up this road, we'll hit the railroad tracks. If we follow them west a ways, we'll hit another road that heads north to I-15. From there, it's less than twenty miles to Barstow. We shouldn't run into any Mexican troops on that freeway."

John was right, there were no Mexican troops on I-15, or in Barstow, but there were Mexicans of another kind: illegal aliens. They were doing more damage than the Mexican army.

Chapter 18

"What do you think is causing all that smoke?" asked Dave pointing towards the low mountains in the distance.

"I've got a bad feeling about this," said Sam. "I think that's Barstow on the other side."

"I wonder what happened," Lisa asked. "Do you think there was a battle there?"

"I'm sure of it," Sam said. "I would be willing to bet that all the major towns along I-40 were hit pretty hard."

"It looks like we're going to pull over," said Dave from the back seat. Sure enough, John pulled off the freeway and into a gas station and just like at the last station, there were signs stuck on the pumps stating that there was no gas available.

Before he got out Sam said, "Everybody stay in the truck until we find out how safe it is here."

John walked up as Sam was getting out. "I'm going to see if anybody's inside. I'd like to find out what the situation is in town, you want to come in with me?"

"You bet I do. I'm not all that crazy about going into town until we know what we're getting into."

When the two of them walked through the door, the slightly overweight, balding, and grandfatherly looking man behind the counter pointed a shotgun at them. "Hold it right there. No Mexicans are allowed in the store so turn around and get out before I shoot you and throw your worthless ass outside for the dogs."

"Are you talking to me?" John asked politely.

"Who the hell do you think I'm talking to? You're the only one in here with dark skin ain't ya?"

"For your information I'm not Mexican, I'm Native American."

"That don't make a difference to me. Hell half the Indians around here joined up with the Mexicans any way."

Sam took a step forward. "So I take it you've had a racial uprising of sorts around here. Whites against Mexicans?"

"Yeah, something like that."

"Well we're just traveling through, headed for Oregon, trying to find someplace safe to stay until all this is settled. You don't need to worry about John here," Sam said patting John on the shoulder, "he used to be in the army and if I wasn't for him, me and my kids wouldn't be here today."

"What did you do in the army?" the man asked, lowering the muzzle of the gun slightly.

"I was in the Rangers," replied John.

The man lowered the gun. "Well if you was in the Rangers I think I can trust you. I was in the Rangers myself a long time ago. By the way, my names Frank."

"So Frank, what can you tell us about the situation in town?" John asked walking toward the counter. "From what we could see it looks like it took quite a pounding. Is all that from the two army's or is part of it from this race war you're talking about?"

"You don't want to go anywhere near town, not if you want to live. True, the American and Mexican army's did a little damage, but most of what you see is from the race war."

Sam said, "You said a lot of the Indians joined forces with the Mexicans, what about the blacks and the Orientals?"

"All of em joined up against the whites. Black, brown, yellow, hell they'd probably let little green men fight on their side. The color of their skin doesn't matter to them, as long as it's not white."

John said, "So is there a way around town that will keep us out of the middle of the fighting?"

"If you head northwest on highway 58, that will take you around most of it, but there's really nowhere that's safe. About a mile down the freeway we have a road block to keep em in town and away from us."

"How many of you are there?" asked Sam.

"There's about a hundred of us, he replied.

John asked, "And how many are in town?"

"I don't know for sure, but if I had to guess I'd say at least four hundred or so."

Sam was shocked there were that many. "Wow, that's a lot."

"Well you've got to remember this is a big agricultural area, most of them are seasonal workers that follow the harvest of crops."

John said, "Yeah and I'll bet 99% are here illegally, too."

"You got that right mister," Frank agreed.

Sam said, "So how come they haven't over run you?"

"I don't know. All we can figure out is that they're so busy fighting among themselves, that they don't have the time or the inclination to try and over run us."

Sam said, "That makes sense. Well, I guess we had better get going if we want to try to get through town before it gets dark. Thanks for the information."

"You're welcome. I'll call Harvey and tell him you're coming and to let you through the road block. If not he's liable to shoot you first and ask questions later," Frank said.

"So what do you think?" Sam asked John. "Do we go through town fast and loud or slow and quiet?"

"Definitely fast and loud. Is there any other way?"

"Sounds good to me," said Sam. His stomach growled and he realized he was hungry. "I think we need to have everybody come in and get something to eat and use the bathroom," he said. "It may be a while before we get another chance."

"That's a good idea," John said, "I'll go tell them."

As John headed out the door, Frank said, "I have some frozen pizzas and burritos that you can nuke in the microwave."

That'll work," said Sam.

* * *

The late afternoon sun was glaring into their eyes when they pulled up to the road block. Sam looked ahead past Richard's vehicle to John's Jeep and watched as a man, Sam assumed it was Harvey, wearing coveralls and carrying a shotgun talked to John. Harvey turned and yelled something that Sam couldn't hear and one of the other men manning the road block walked over and got into one of the two trucks that were blocking the road. He backed it up just enough for a vehicle to squeeze through. Harvey waved at Sam as he drove through the gap and Sam threw him a salute.

John set a blistering pace down the empty road and they were making good time.

Sam was glad to see that they didn't have to go directly through Barstow. Instead they were on a road that curved to the north and was separated from the town itself by a set of railroad tracks and a large dry wash. Sam realized this was a nice buffer zone between them and the bad guys.

Lisa was looking towards town, shaking her head. "Would you look at all the destruction those guys have done to that town."

"It's a shame…" Sam started to say when he was interrupted by an explosion a couple of blocks away.

"Do you think that was a gas station?" asked Dave from the back seat.

Sam thought for a moment. "I don't know for sure, but if I had to guess, I'd say it was probably a car or a truck. It wasn't big enough for anything like a gas station."

"Unbelievable," muttered Lisa.

Sam just nodded. They were almost to the end of town and he was starting to think that they were going to make it through without having any problems. Then his phone rang. Flipping it open he hit talk, then speaker phone.

"You know I'm getting to where I don't want to answer this thing anymore. It seems like every time you call me it's bad news," he said.

John's voice boomed out, "Have everybody lock and load buddy, we've got company up here and no way to avoid them. We may have to shoot our way out of here."

"You heard him," Sam said turning serious. "Let's get ready."

"What's the situation John?" Sam asked as Lisa, Dave, and Ashley pulled out their guns and made sure they were loaded.

"There's a road block ahead of us forcing us to turn left and as you can see we have to cross the rail road tracks in order to get to the main highway. Unfortunately, the bad guys have a road block set up there, too."

"What about going right?" Sam asked hopefully.

"Not an option. It's a dirt road and there's a tractor parked on it."

"What about just plowing thru?"

"I think we'd be better off talking to them first. You never know, maybe they'll be nice and let us through, if not we can always shoot our way out," John said.

"Shit," Sam swore, hoping it didn't come down to a

shootout. "Okay I'll leave my phone on and follow your lead."

He was close enough now that he could see the road block on the tracks. He watched as John's Jeep turned and slowly made its way to the vehicles blocking the road.

Sam closed up the gap between him and Richard, not knowing if he should or not. He wasn't sure if they would be better off spread out a little or bunched up.

Deciding it probably didn't matter, he set his phone in the drink holder where he could still hear it. He opened the center console and took out his pistol. Flipping the safety off, he held it in his lap pointed at the door. With his left hand he pushed the buttons and rolled down all of the windows. If they needed to shoot, he didn't want the windows in the way.

"Daddy, I'm scared," Ashley whimpered from the back seat.

"I know Ash, I am, too."

Looking in his rearview mirror, he saw the cars that had been blocking the road were now coming up behind him. He could faintly hear John's voice on the phone, talking to someone, but he couldn't hear what he was saying. He tried to see what was going on at John's Jeep, all he could see was four gangster looking youths walking up to Richard's SUV, two on each side.

Sam saw movement behind him. He looked in his mirror and saw four tough looking youths getting out of the cars that had pulled up behind the truck. They split up, two coming up his side, the other two going to the passenger side. Then four quick shots rang out and over the phone he heard John yell, "*Now! Now! Now!*"

At the sound of the shots, the four youths walking up to the truck lifted their guns and rushed forward. The one closest to Sam's door yelled, "Kill the white honky trash."

Sam stuck his gun out the window and fired two quick shots. At the same time, he heard Dave's pistol going off next to him and both gangsters fell to the ground. He could hear the roar of Lisa's shotgun and the smaller pop of Ashley's pistol. He looked towards Richard's Jeep only to see it quickly pulling away from him. He smashed his foot down on the gas pedal and the truck surged forward. Two of the youths who had been standing by Richard's Jeep were sprawled out on the left side of the road, the other two ran in front of the truck, firing their guns. The windshield spider webbed as multiple bullets punched through it, sending small shards of glass flying through the cab.

Sam felt something slam into his left shoulder, shoving him back in his seat.

Disbelief that he had been shot was the first thing that flashed through his mind.

Then panic and fear welled up in him, but it was quickly replaced by anger. In a blind rage, he turned the steering wheel and plowed into the two youths.

"*Screw you!*" he screamed out as they disappeared under the truck.

Then the truck flashed past a car that looked like it had been pushed out of the road by someone. Sam assumed John did it since he was the lead vehicle when they pulled up to the roadblock.

As they flew over the railroad tracks and onto the main highway, he checked his mirror to make sure no one was following them.

"Dave, Ashley, are you two okay?' he asked over his shoulder.

Dave was the only one to answer. "I think so."

"What about you Ashley," he asked her again.

"*You lied to me,*" she shouted.

Shocked at the outburst, Sam turned and took a quick look at her, wincing at the pain it caused him.

"What are you talking about?" he said leaning forward to ease the pain.

"Don't you remember the talk we had when you told us that you and mom were getting a divorce?"

"Yes, I remember," he said, fighting off the black fog that was wrapping itself around him, pulling him into unconsciousness.

"Do you remember what you told me about killing Mexican's?"

"Oh, yeah, I remember now," he whispered as the fog closed in more. "I told you that you wouldn't have to shoot anybody."

"No, you *promised* me that I wouldn't have to shoot anybody. You LIED to me, and now I'm a murderer," she wailed.

"You're not a murderer Sweetheart. You only did what you had to do to save yourself, and us," he mumbled as the blackness slowly closed in on him.

From somewhere in the fog, he heard Lisa say, "Sam, are you okay? Oh my god, you're bleeding. Dave I need...."

Then everything went black.

Chapter 19

"Dave, I need your help," Lisa yelled. Instinctively, she grabbed the steering wheel as Sam slumped forward, his foot still on the pedal, sending the truck careening across the road.

Dave reached over the seat and grabbed the collar of Sam's shirt. He pulled him off the steering wheel and back against the seat.

Before Lisa could correct the path of the truck, it took out a sign that read:

Thank You For Visiting Barstow
We Hope You Enjoyed You're Stay
Drive Safely And Come Back Soon

She pushed the shift lever up into neutral and let the truck slow down on its own until it came to a stop. She shut off the key and let out a sigh of relief, but she couldn't relax. She needed to get a hold of Richard.

Dave jumped out of the truck and threw open Sam's door. "What do you need me to do?" He looked from Lisa to the blood oozing from his father's shoulder.

"Help me find his phone," Lisa said. "We need to get Richard back here."

Ashley leaned over the back seat with tears running down her cheeks. "It's right there . . . in the cup holder."

As Lisa picked up the phone, John's voice blasted out of the speaker. "Sam, what the hell are you doing back there?" he demanded. "That isn't a good place to stop."

Trying to keep her voice from quivering, Lisa said,

"John, Sam's been shot. Can you get Richard back here as soon as possible?"

"We'll be right there."

Lisa flipped the phone closed and put her hand on Ashley's arm. "Don't worry, Ash. He's going to be okay. As soon as Richard gets here, he'll fix him up as good as new."

"I hope so. I don't want to lose my dad, too."

Lisa turned to Dave. "Why don't you see if you can find a towel or something that we can put over the wound. We need to slow down the bleeding."

While Dave went to get a towel, Lisa flipped up the center console and knelt on the seat. Reaching over, she gently unbuttoned Sam's shirt. "Ashley, do you think you could help me? I need to get his shirt off so we can see what we're doing."

"What do you want me to do?" Ashley said, wiping the tears off her face.

"I need you to push him forward a little bit."

Ashley put her hands on the back of Sam's shoulders and pushed.

"*Ahhhh*," Sam moaned, pulling away from the pressure Ashley had applied to the exit wound on his back.

"Oh, God, I'm sorry Dad," Ashley sobbed as she jerked her hands back. "I didn't mean to hurt you."

"It's okay, Ash," said Lisa. "He's still unconscious. Bring your hands over this way a little more and let's try it again." She pointed to a spot away from the wound.

Ashley's hands shook as she placed them gently on his back again and pushed.

Lisa started to pull the shirt down when Dave said, "Wouldn't it be easier to cut it off?" He held up a pair of scissors.

Feeling foolish for not thinking of doing that in the

first place, Lisa sheepishly replied, "You're right, it would be easier. Thanks." She took the scissors and started cutting away Sam's blood-soaked shirt. Hearing a vehicle approach, she feared to look up. She said to Dave, "Please, tell me that's John and Richard."

He said stoically, "Yes, it's them." He yelled, "Hurry, Richard."

Lisa heard doors slamming and feet stomping across the pavement.

Richard's body filled the opening of the door. "What have we got here?" He leaned in and looked at Sam's chest. "Mmmm, this doesn't look that serious. The bullet passed under the collar bone. I don't think it hit anything major." He winked at Lisa. "I'll have him back slapping people around in no time at all."

"Are you sure it's not serious?" asked Ashley, shaking in the back seat.

He opened his medical bag. "Of course, you should know me well enough by now to know that I wouldn't lie to you."

Lisa winced at his mention of the word *lie* and wondered if it made Ashley regret so harshly accusing her father of lying.

From behind Richard, John said, "I hate to put any more pressure on you, Richard, but is there any way you can work on him as we're traveling? We're not far from Barstow and I would really like to put some distance between us and the bad guys."

"Well, I suppose if Ashley wouldn't mind riding with Jean, I could lay him out on the back seat and keep him stable until we get somewhere safe to work on him."

Jean offered, "Why don't we take him to the Air Force base that's just up the road?"

"Edwards Air Force Base," stated John. "It's only about fifteen miles from here."

"That's a good idea," Richard replied. "They should have a hospital, or at least a clinic where I can work on him."

"Well then, let's get going," Lisa said sharply as she nervously looked back at the town. She didn't want another encounter that would strand them helplessly out on these open roads.

Richard, John, and Dave, carefully moved Sam to the back seat.

Ashley quietly sobbed in Lisa's arms.

Jean and Sunshine cleaned up the blood the best they could.

"Are you driving or am I?" Dave asked Lisa as Jean led Ashley away.

"You drive," Lisa said, feeling some relief that she wouldn't have to concentrate on the road. "I'm too upset."

As they pulled out, Lisa looked over her shoulder at Sam's unconscious form. Her heart ached for him. Her mind went to Shawn and how he had died so suddenly when he had broken his neck. How could she face losing another man that she had learned to love? Only now, looking at Sam in his helpless condition, did she realize the depth of her love for him. She had seen the soft side of Sam's heart with his concern for his family, and she had seen the tough side that forged on through the dangers. Until now, she hadn't realized how much she had counted on him to get them through all of this . . . and to be together with him in Oregon when it was over. She sighed and turned back to face the road. She closed her eyes. *Just make him okay, God, that's all I ask.*

* * *

Feeling anxious and pressed to get more help for Sam, Lisa shifted forward in her seat as Dave, driving in the lead, pulled up to the main guard shack.

Dave put the truck in park as a harried-looking M.P., an M-16 slung across his chest, walked toward him with a *not-again* look on his face. "No civilians are allowed . . ."

"My dad's been shot and needs immediate medical attention," Dave blurted, pointing to the back seat.

The M.P. stopped, stepped back, and lifted his gun. "Hands in the air, now."

Three more M.P.s ran out of the shack and pointed their guns at the truck.

"What the hell?" Lisa stammered, completely stunned at the sudden change in their behavior.

"They saw our guns," Richard shouted from the back seat. He put his hands on top of the seat. "Put your hands up where they can see them. And whatever you do, don't reach for a gun."

Dave, eyes wide, kept his hands on the steering wheel.

Lisa quickly put hers on the dash.

The M.P. said, "Driver, open your door and step out. Keep your hands where I can see them at all times."

Dave reached down to shut the key off.

"*Hands*," yelled the M.P. "I need to see your hands or I will open fire."

"It's okay," Lisa said, seeing the uncertainty on Dave's face. "Leave it running."

Using the outside handle, Dave opened his door and climbed out.

An M.P. cuffed him.

Another said, "Now, each of you get out, one at a time. Lady first."

When Lisa got out, she glanced back at the rest of their party. They were also required to get out of their vehicles and were handcuffed.

When everyone had been cuffed and spread-eagle against the hood of the vehicles, one of the M.P.s yelled, "We have an injured man here." While five M.P.s held guns on them, another ten or twelve moved around the vehicles.

Standing in the dirt and heat, Lisa faced the truck, but watched the men from the corner of her eye. Her anger started to get the best of her as she worried about Sam's condition.

"So, Captain," a domineering voice called out, "what's the story with these people?"

"We don't know yet, sir. All we know at this point is that we have three vehicles, numerous weapons, and eight people, one of whom has been shot."

Looking over her shoulder, Lisa saw a tall, middle-aged man with a crew cut. He wore combat fatigues with two general stars on his shoulders.

Unable to contain herself any longer, Lisa turned around. "If you would let me, I'm sure I could explain our situation, sir."

"Later," he said abruptly, holding up a hand to refrain her from speaking. "I really would like to know why you're trying to smuggle weapons onto a U.S. military base, but right now, you're all under arrest for aiding and abating the Mexican Army and attempted sabotage."

"What?" she cried out, taking a step forward. "You've got to be kidding. We're not . . . "

"Silence," roared the general, pointing his finger at her face.

"Let it go for now, Lisa," Richard said as he glared at the general. "We'll get it straightened out later."

Glaring back, the general bellowed, "Take them to the brig, Captain. I'll interrogate them after we've had a chance to search their vehicles."

Lisa had the distinct feeling that something wasn't right with the general. She wasn't sure why, but she didn't trust him.

As she was taken away, she glanced back at the truck and worried about what would happen to Sam. She wanted to scream at the stupid M.P.s and their stupid general for playing games with them and putting Sam's life further at risk.

* * *

Hours later, as she sat in the cell with Jean, Sunshine, and Ashley, Lisa's emotions had run the gauntlet from anger and frustration to apprehension and fear. Now, she was just plain pissed. At least, they had removed the cuffs from their wrists. For the tenth time in the last hour, she got off the cot and walked to the metal door. Putting her back to it, she kicked it with the heel of her cowboy boot. The sound of the heel banging on the door echoed down the hallway and bounced off the concrete walls and floors.

"Do you have to keep doing that?" Ashley asked from the cot, where she sat with Sunshine's arm around her shoulders. "It's not doing any good. Nobody's come yet, and I doubt if they will until they're ready."

"I'm going to keep doing it until somebody comes and tells me what's going on. I don't know about you, but I'd like to know how your dad's doing."

"Me, too, but you're driving me nuts with all that banging."

Lisa heard footsteps coming down the hall. She turned around. "Well, it seems as though my banging has finally gotten someone's attention. Now, maybe we can find out what's going on."

A key rattled in the lock and the door swung open,

revealing two young soldiers.

"You," said the one in the doorway as he pointed at Lisa, "come with us."

Escorting her on both sides, they took her down a long hall to a heavy wooden door. Opening the door, they shoved her inside.

"Sit down," said the big general from behind a large metal desk.

Seeing only one other chair, sitting right in front of the desk, Lisa slowly walked to the desk. "I'll answer your questions if you'll answer mine." She put her hands on the desk and leaned forward. "How is Sam . . . my friend that was shot?"

"Your accomplice is fine. He's being held in a cell with the others. Now, sit down."

Accomplice? "So, I assume you're still under the assumption that we're helping the Mexicans?" she asked, standing straight and folding her arms across her chest in a show of defiance.

Slamming his hand down on the desk with every word, he yelled, "*I . . . said . . . sit . . . down.*"

She waivered, wondering if acting defiant was the best tact to take with this man, or if she would get more out of him by acting submissive. She found she couldn't read him. With a sigh, she pulled out the chair and lowered herself into it. Crossing her legs, as if she was in a board meeting in Manhattan, she smoothed the imaginary wrinkles out of her jeans. Looking him in the eye, she said, "Okay, I'm sitting down. Now what?"

"First, I need your name."

"Lisa Baldwin, and you are?" she demanded.

"I am General Dawson, commander of this base," he said with a haughty, better-than-thou attitude. "Now that we have the introductions out of the way, I want you to tell me why you and your *friends* were trying to smuggle guns onto a U.S. military base. Are you working with the Mexican army in an attempt to overthrow the American government?"

"That's ridiculous. Of course, we're not."

"Then, tell me why you're here?"

"I assume you've talked to John and Richard. Didn't they tell you?"

He leaned forward in his chair and glared at her. "Yes, they did, but I'm not sure I believe them. I want to hear you're version of the story."

Feeling frustrated, she sighed. After a brief hesitation, she gave him her condensed version of what had happened, from the time the earthquake had hit until they had pulled up to the gate.

The general didn't say a word. Occasionally, he would write something down on the pad in front of him or nod his head. When she was done, he hollered, "Private."

The door swung open and one of the soldiers walked in. "Yes, sir?"

"Take her back to her cell and bring in the next one."

"Wait a minute," she said as the soldier approached her chair. "Don't you believe me?"

"So far, you and your friends have all told me basically the same story," he said tapping his pencil on the pad of paper. "Which is why I'm not sure I believe it. It's too perfect."

Lisa stood up. "Believe what you want, but we're telling you the truth." Turning on her heel, she marched out of the room with an angry step.

* * *

Two days later, Lisa furiously paced back and forth across the twenty-by-twenty concrete floor. "I don't understand why they're still keeping us locked up in here.

We've told them, twice now, what happened to us, and they still don't believe it."

Sunshine and Ashley had both remained sullen and quiet since their meeting with the general. Jean, on the other hand, didn't seem affected by anything that had happened. She lay on her cot as though having a pleasant afternoon rest.

"How can you just sit there or lie there and do nothing?" Lisa demanded of the others as she stood in the middle of the cell. "Aren't you worried about what's going to happen?"

"Of course, we are," Jean admitted, "but it doesn't do any good to fret about it."

"And besides," Sunshine added, "what can we do?"

"I don't know, but I feel like I need to do something." She walked to the door and looked through the six-inch window. She kicked the door and spun around. "I hate being cooped up in here and not knowing what's going on."

She walked to her cot, flopped down, and faced the wall. Her mind, in overdrive, created numerous scenarios of what was going to happen to them. Some were deadly, some just plain silly. Her mind whirled in a never-ending movie of possible outcomes. Finally, she drifted off into a dreamland of angry Mexicans shouting racial slurs and demented generals torturing innocent citizens in dark, dank dungeons.

Chapter 20

Sam slowly opened his eyes, squinting in the harsh glare of the florescent bulbs recessed in the ceiling. Turning his head, he looked around the room.

Dave lay on a cot facing the wall.

Richard sat watching Sam from another cot. "So, how's the shoulder feeling?" asked Richard as he stood up and stretched.

Sitting up and swinging his feet to the floor, Sam carefully touched the bandage on his left shoulder. "It hurts like hell."

"Let me take a look," Richard said. "I want to make sure it's not getting infected."

With Richard's help, Sam carefully removed the camouflage shirt someone had given him. "Ouch," he yelped as Richard poked and prodded a tender spot.

"Oh, quit being a sissy." Richard ruffled Sam's hair.

"I can't help it. When it comes to pain, I am a sissy. By the way, where's John?"

"About an hour ago, a guard showed up and said the general wanted to talk to him again."

"I don't suppose you've heard anything about the women?" Sam asked as Richard reapplied the bandage to his shoulder.

"No, we haven't. I asked the general about them yesterday. He told me it was none of my concern. I've got to admit, when he said that, I wanted to pull him out from behind that desk and beat the hell out of him."

"I know what you mean. I don't know about you, but I have the distinct feeling that the general's not playing with a full deck."

"He's not." Richard returned to his cot and sat down. "He's exhibiting all the classic symptoms of a paranoid-schizophrenic. He thinks everybody's trying to sabotage the base, or that they're working with the Mexicans. I think the stress of his job finally sent him over the edge."

"He scared the hell out of me," Dave said, stretching out on his cot. "I half-expected him to take me to a dungeon and torture me."

Sam chuckled and nodded. He had had the same expectations. "By the way, Richard, I've been meaning to ask, what kind of doctor are you?"

"I'm a pediatrician," he proudly stated.

"You're a pediatrician?" Dave sputtered in disbelief.

Richard looked hurt. "Is that so hard to believe?"

Sam laughed. "Well, I've got to admit, the mental image that just flashed through my mind is kind of funny."

"Yeah," Dave said, joining Sam's laughter. "How many kids started screaming and crying when you walked into the exam room and saw you for the first time?"

Richard chuckled. "Not as many as you'd think. I actually have a way with kids. And besides, most of my patients are young enough that they don't have the society-imposed fear of a large black man that possess a lot of adults."

Sam came alert when he heard the door opening.

John walked into the cell. "Okay, fellow jailbirds, it's time to spread your wings and fly away. We're out-a here."

Sam jumped to his feet. He winced at the pain the move caused to his shoulder. "Are you serious?" Deep down, he couldn't help think this was a cruel practical joke, and that, in reality, they were going to be held captive forever.

"I'm dead serious," John said staunchly. "I finally convinced the general to let me make a phone call. Once I did, things happened fast."

"The women, too?" asked Richard. His concern for Jean showed in his voice.

"Yes, in fact, they're being released as we speak."

"How did you pull this off?" Sam asked.

"I'll tell you in a little while. Right now, we need to meet up with the girls in the cafeteria."

Having nothing to gather up, they left the cell and were escorted to the cafeteria by two soldiers.

"Daddy," Ashley cried. She jumped up and rushed to him. Being careful not to hurt his shoulder, she hugged his chest. Her voice, muffled by his shirt, said, "I was so worried about you. They wouldn't tell me if you were okay or not." She pulled away and looked into his eyes. With tears falling down her cheeks and trembling lips, she asked, "You are okay, aren't you?"

"I'm fine, sweetheart." He pulled her close. "Are you okay? They didn't hurt you did they?"

"No, I'm fine."

As Sam held his daughter, he looked at Lisa.

She gave him a smile and a wink.

Sam heard the door on the other side of the room open. Keeping his right arm draped protectively over Ashley's shoulders, he turned to see three soldiers walking towards them.

Lisa, standing on one side of Sam, slipped her hand into his.

He gently squeezed and gave her a quick smile. She warmed his heart. He felt so grateful she had come along.

The rest of the party . . . Dave, Richard, Jean, John, and Sunshine . . . stood firmly around them.

Sam felt proud to have such loyal friends at his side.

A tall, gray-haired soldier stopped in front of them. "I

am General Thomas, and I would like to apologize for the way you have been treated. I want you all to know that I am now commander of this base. General Dawson has been temporarily relieved of his command and ordered to undergo a psychological evaluation."

"So, what about us?" asked Sam. "Are we free to go?"

"Yes, you are. And if there's anything you need, let Captain Wilson here know." He pointed to the man on his left. "We'll be glad to give it to you."

"What about our vehicles?" Sam asked.

"All your vehicles have been checked over by our mechanics. They fixed everything they could, including the shattered windshield and missing mirror of your truck, Sam."

"Thanks," Sam replied, feeling a sense of relief that they're vehicles would be in good shape for the next portion of their journey.

Lisa said, "You really had a windshield for his truck here?"

General Thomas laughed. "You wouldn't believe what we have on this base. And some of it, you wouldn't want to know about."

"The first thing I want is a long, hot shower," said Richard.

"We have private quarters ready," said the Captain. "You can stay as long as you want."

"Thank you," said Sam. "I think one night should be long enough to get ready. One thing we could use is information about what's going on north of here. We're thinking of heading toward Oregon. I don't really want to get into another situation like the one in Barstow."

"We'll fill you in on everything later," said General Thomas, looking at his watch. "I'm sorry, but I need to go." He shook his head and grimaced. "You wouldn't believe what a mess General Dawson made of this base."

As he walked away, he called out, "By the way, I would like all of you to join me for dinner tonight at six."

"That sounds good to us," said John, getting nods of agreement from everyone.

"If you would follow me," said Captain Wilson, "I'll show you to your quarters."

* * *

The afternoon sun felt warm on Sam's face as Captain Wilson led the group out of the cafeteria to three topless Jeeps. "If you would follow me in these two Jeeps, I'll take you to your quarters now." He indicated two of the Jeeps with a wave of his hand.

Dave and Ashley climbed into the back seat, and Sam headed for the driver's side.

"Not so fast," Lisa said, heading him off. "You're hurt and shouldn't be driving." She gave him a gentle shove towards the passenger's side.

Irritated that she was taking control, he said, "I can drive . . . "

"Don't argue with me," she barked, putting her hands on her hips and glaring at him.

"*Sam,*" Richard yelled from the back of the other Jeep, "as your doctor, I'm ordering you to get in the passenger's seat and let Lisa drive."

"But I . . . "

"You'd better let her drive, Dad," Ashley said, winking at Dave, "or Richard may have to patch you up again."

"Yeah, Dad," Dave said. "You don't have to be in control all the time. Let her drive once in a while."

Embarrassed to have his control issues brought up in front of everyone, Sam relented and climbed into the passenger's seat.

With a look of triumph on her face, Lisa hopped in. "Better buckle up," she said, looking serious. "I've never driven a stick shift before."

Remembering his first time driving a stick, with all the jerky starts and stops, Sam fumbled with his seat belt, trying to get it done up before Lisa started the Jeep.

Leaning over his seat, Ashley helped him.

"Thanks," he said over his shoulder.

Lisa slipped the Jeep into first and smoothly let out the clutch.

Sam realized he'd been had. "Never driven a stick before, huh?"

"What can I say, I'm a fast learner." She smiled and shifted into second gear.

Sam laughed and leaned back in his seat.

Lisa followed the other Jeeps across the base until Captain Wilson came to a residential area. He turned down a tree-lined street and stopped in front of a two-story brick house. Sam's truck sat in the driveway, while John's and Richard's vehicles had been parked in the driveway of the house next door.

Captain Wilson stood up in his Jeep. "Sam, Lisa, and the kids are in this house. You other four are in that one." He pointed to the other house. "I'll give you a little while to get settled, then I'll come back and get you for dinner." He spun the Jeep around and drove off, leaving them on their own.

Sam studied the house. "When Captain Wilson said he had private quarters ready for us, he wasn't kidding."

While he retrieved clean clothing out of the truck, Sam wondered how many bedrooms the house would have available and who might have to share. He was relieved to find four bedrooms and two baths.

When they came to the master bathroom, Lisa said, "Ladies before gentlemen." She walked into the room and shut the door.

Ashley made a beeline for the other shower.

"That's okay," Dave said. "I can wait."

"I just hope they don't use all the hot water," Sam said, putting his good arm around Dave's shoulders and leading him into the living room to wait their turn for the showers.

* * *

Setting down his fork, Sam let out a sigh. He didn't think he could eat another bite. He hadn't had a delicious, full-course meal that good in a long time. The general had gone all out for their last dinner: porter-house steaks, baked potatoes with chives and sour cream, steamed broccoli and cauliflower, fresh-baked rolls smothered in real butter, and, for dessert, a chocolate cake with vanilla frosting with coffee or hot chocolate to drink.

When everyone finished eating and sipped their drinks, Sam said, "General, what's going on with the war? Are you winning?"

"Our armed forces are making significant headway against the Mexicans." He put his coffee cup down. "We determined that the invasion was a spur-of-the-moment act by the Mexican president, and his army wasn't prepared for this kind of war."

Richard removed a toothpick from his mouth. "What do you mean by *this kind of war*?"

"The Mexicans were prepared to fight our army, but when the citizens stood up and fought back, it overwhelmed them. They didn't have the manpower to fight in return."

Sam only heard half what the general was saying as he watched Lisa lick the frosting off the corner of her mouth. Her tongue slid up one side of her lips, then the other, in a slow, sensual movement that Sam found slightly erotic.

She caught him staring and stuck her tongue out, ruining the fantasy running through his mind. She turned to the general. "So, with the help of the American people, you're winning?"

The general laughed. "We would have won anyway, but I won't deny that we do appreciate all the help we've gotten from our loyal citizens."

John said, "How long do you think it will be before I can return to my home on the desert?"

The general looked thoughtful for a moment. "It's going to be at least a couple of weeks, maybe even a month before we get that area of Arizona cleared out. We want to make sure it's completely safe before we send people back to their homes."

John put his arm around Sunshine. "Well, I guess we'll have to go north for a while."

"That's okay," she said as she snuggled closer. "We've been talking about taking a vacation anyway. This way, we don't have a choice."

At the mention of their intended route, Sam forgot about Lisa's sensual tongue and turned his attention back to the general. "That reminds me . . . what can you tell us about the situation north of here?"

"A small race war, like the one in Barstow, has broken out on Highways 5 and 99. You're going to have to detour to Highway 394 when you get to the town of Boron. I've marked it out on this map." He handed the map to Sam. "I know it takes you out of your way, but there's no other way to get to Oregon."

Sam looked at the map. "This takes us clear over to Reno," he complained.

John said, "Are you sure we can't go up Highway 5 or 99. How bad could it be?"

"Pretty bad," the general said in a tone of regret. "These little race wars are hard to control. But we're handling them as carefully and diplomatically as possible. As it stands right now, we feel that once we've pushed the Mexican army back across the border, the situation here will likely fizzle out and return to normal."

"So, in other words," Richard growled, "you aren't going to do anything. You're going to sit back and contain the violence and hope the fighting ends on its own."

"That's right," the general stated flatly. "Do you have a problem with that?"

"As a matter of fact, I do," Richard retorted. "Have you given any thought to all the innocent people, like us, who will be injured or killed while you're *handling things*?"

The general's face turned hard. His eyes filled with fire as he glared across the silent table at Richard. "I can assure you," he said with force, "we are doing everything we can to diminish casualties.

Not wanting the general and Richard to get into a major debate, Sam interjected, "What can you tell us about the area around Reno?"

Returning to his more jovial self, the general sat back in his chair. "Reno and the surrounding areas have been overrun by refugees. The hotels are overflowing, and the casinos have shut down until order is restored."

Lisa said, "If we go to Reno, where are we going to stay?"

The general shook his head. "Once you leave here, you're chances of finding a place to stay are slim to none. My suggestion would be to take camping gear and rough it."

Dave piped up enthusiastically, "We have a tent and sleeping bags."

Richard groaned at the mention of sleeping in a tent.

"Yeah, we do," Sam agreed, "but our camping gear is for warm weather. Remember, it's winter and, when we leave here, we'll climb in elevation. It's going to get colder. I don't think our gear is going to do us much good."

"We have some arctic gear you can take with you," the general offered. "With some good tents and sleeping bags, you should be able to survive for a few nights."

John looked around the group. "I'm sure we'll be fine. We'll have to make do. If Reno is as bad as you say, we don't have a choice."

Jean sat up in her chair. "What about after we leave Reno? Can you tell us what it's like in Southern Oregon and Northern California?"

"That's a good question," Lisa said, looking at the general for a response.

"Basically, the same as Reno," he said staunchly. "The Northwest, from here to Calgary, Canada, has been overrun with refugees. The larger cities, like Portland, San Francisco, and Seattle, are handling it better than the smaller towns, which don't have the infrastructure to deal with so many people. Water and food are their main concerns at the moment. We're doing everything we can to ship food in, but we're not keeping up with the demand. Yesterday, a convoy of four trucks was ambushed, the drivers killed, and all the food was stolen."

"Who would do something like that?" Sunshine demanded.

The general shook his head. "You've got to remember, there are millions of people who've been forced to flee, not only the volcano and the ash cloud, but also the Mexican invasion. People are living in their cars, in tents, wherever they can. And they're desperate."

"And most of these people," John added, "are from

cities and don't know how to survive in this type of situation. If they can't run down to the store and buy food like they are used to, they'll get it somehow, even if it means ambushing trucks."

"That's right," the general stated. "Your average person doesn't have the knowledge to endure for more than a few days in a survival situation. You, on the other hand, can and will survive. With John's military background, Sam's outdoor experience, and Richard's and Jean's medical backgrounds, you've got enough experience between all of you to get through this."

"He's right," Lisa said brightly. "We'll get through this, but only if we stick together."

From the end of the table, Ashley said softly, "Do we have to go to Oregon? Isn't there somewhere else we could go that isn't having problems?"

Sam looked at her worried face. "Our only other choice would be south or east. How's the situation in the rest of the country, General?"

The general took another sip of his coffee and nodded his head. "Pretty good, Sam. Everything east of the Mississippi is normal. The Midwest is the only area we had to evacuate, and some of those people are already starting to return to their homes. It turns out that the volcano eruption wasn't as large as first reported."

Ashley's eyes darkened with a questioning look. "Does that mean we didn't need to leave our home?"

"No," the general said bluntly. "Everything within four hundred miles of Yellowstone is covered in ash. Your home in Buffalo is buried under about ten feet of ash. You'll never be able to live there again."

Sam knew what Ashley had been thinking, that if they wouldn't have left home, her mother would still be alive. He smiled at her, letting her know he was thinking about Linda, too.

Dave fidgeted in his seat. "What about going south, to Florida or Georgia?"

General Thomas shook his head again. "There's no way to get there safely. You'd have to go through the same country you just came across, and you know how dangerous that was. Your best bet is to go north for now. If you decide to relocate later, you can." He stood up. "I wish I could stay here and visit with you longer, but I have some things I need to attend to."

Sam stood up to shake his hand. "Thank you for all your help."

"You're welcome, I'll see you all in the morning." He walked out of the room.

* * *

Sunshine stretched. "If we're going to get an early start, we'd better get to bed."

"I agree," said Jean, getting up from the table. "I can't wait to sleep in a *real* bed, instead of a cot."

"Wait a minute," Richard said, "there's something I need to know first." He turned to John. "It's time to come clean. How did you manage to get us released?"

"There's really nothing to explain. I just convinced General Dawson to let me make a phone call."

"You called your dad, didn't you?" Lisa said with a knowing smile.

"Who's your dad?" Sam asked.

"Well, technically, he's not my dad. He's my stepdad."

"Who the hell is he?" demanded Richard.

All eyes focused on John with curiosity.

"Senator Howard Barker," said John.

"As in Speaker-of-the-House Senator Barker?" sputtered Richard.

"Yeah, but I try not to let too many people know. It seems like, as soon they find out I'm related to him, they want to know if I can tell him this or that. Or, they try to convince me to get him to give a speech at some benefit their organization is throwing."

Sam laughed. "Well, I for one am glad that you've got connections. If not, who knows how long we would have been stuck here?"

As they walked out of the dining hall, Sam put his arm around Lisa.

She smiled up at him with her sparkling blue eyes.

Things are looking up. He smiled back, then he thought back to the last night they'd spent at John's house. "Lisa, can I ask you something?"

"Sure, what's on your mind?"

"Our last night at John's house, I heard you and Ashley talking . . . "

She pulled away from him. Her eyes wide in surprise, she blurted, "You heard what we were talking about?"

"Well, not everything, just one word: *marriage.* What were you two talking about?"

Lisa laughed and visibly relaxed. "She said it was okay with her and Dave if we got married."

In mock horror, he stammered, "*What? Married? Us?*"

"Relax." She patted his chest with her hand. "I told her that, even though there were feelings between us, nether one of us is ready for that yet."

"What makes you think I'll ever be ready?" he asked.

"Call it women's intuition," she replied, giving him a wink.

"I can't deny my feelings for you," he admitted. "And I'm pretty sure you have feelings for me, too. So, how about when we get to Oregon, we go out to dinner and talk about it."

"Are you asking me out on a date?" Lisa asked, coyly

fluttering her eyelashes at him.

He laughed. "Yeah, I guess I am."

"It's a start," she said, putting her arm around his waist and walking close to him on their way to the Jeep.

Chapter 21

The closer they got to Reno, the more uneasy and restless Lisa felt. She didn't know why she felt so unsettled, but she sensed something bad was about to happen. She didn't know what it was or how to prevent it. *Maybe it's because we're getting closer to Oregon, and Sam and I will talk more about our relationship.* She glanced at him.

He smiled at her.

No, she liked where they were. That wasn't what bothered her. She wondered if it could be the kids she was worried about. Taking on two teenage step-kids would be a big responsibility. Still, she'd been getting along with them pretty well over the last few days and felt confident that wasn't the problem. For the moment, she pushed the sense of foreboding to the back of her mind so she could help Sam negotiate through the heavy traffic as they came to the outskirts of Carson City.

General Thomas had been right about Carson City and Reno. Both were crowded with people and vehicles. Everywhere Lisa looked, she saw campers, trailers, and motor homes. Parking lots, parks, and even private residences were filled to over-flowing and, still, the vehicles kept coming. The traffic on the freeway reminded her of rush hour in L.A. It moved so slowly. It was impossible to find a free space in which to park.

State Troopers and National Guard soldiers forced Sam to stay on the freeway and pass straight through both towns.

About ten miles north of Reno, Sam exited the

freeway behind John's Jeep. A trooper directed them to a dry lakebed with numerous parked RVs. A light dusting of snow covered the alkali flats, turning the alkali into a gooey, sticky mess. The afternoon sun broke through the clouds, just enough to highlight the mountains to the west.

Finding a place on the outer edge of the lakebed, Sam pulled in and parked.

Ashley slid out of the rear seat. "This place reminds me of that town in Colorado we stopped . . . where those men broke that poor guy's arm."

Dave walked around the truck. "What was that place called? Mont . . . something."

"Montrose," Sam said as he arched his back, stretching his muscles.

Lisa pulled her coat tighter. The hair on the back of her neck stood up. She shivered, but not from the cold. She glanced around nervously. Nothing seemed amiss, but she sensed someone was watching her. "For some reason, this place is different. It seems more calm and orderly," she lied, not wanting Sam to know how she really felt.

"That may be," Sam said as he opened up the back of the truck, "but we still need to be on-guard so nothing bad happens."

"I agree," Richard said, approaching with Jean, John, and Sunshine.

Sam looked directly at Lisa. "The same rules apply here as back in Colorado. Use the buddy system if you leave the truck."

Lisa smiled and nodded in agreement.

Everyone pitched in and helped set up the tents.

Sam said, "Why don't Lisa, Dave, Ashley and I share one tent and Richard, Jean, John, and Sunshine can share the other one.

"I think we should all pile into one tent," Richard said as he handed a sleeping bag to Sunshine, inside the tent helping Jean lay out their beds.

"Why?" Sunshine asked.

"More body heat to keep me warm. I'm going to freeze to death tonight."

John chuckled. "You're not going to freeze. In fact, I'll bet you sleep better tonight than you did in that army cot in our cell at Edwards."

Lisa noticed the concern in Richard's eyes. "Haven't you ever camped out, Richard?"

"Are you kidding? The closest I've came to camping out was sleeping in line while waiting to get Grateful Dead tickets back in my college days."

"You'll do just fine," Sam said as he unloaded the last of the equipment from the truck. "Keep your clothes on and burrow down next to Jean. Your combined body heat will have you throwing covers off in no time."

"That sounds interesting," Richard said, lifting his brows and slipping an arm around Jean's waist as she came out of the tent.

She shoved him away, barely moving his bulk. "Remember, there's going to be other people in the tent with us, so don't get any romantic ideas in your head."

Ashley tapped Lisa on the shoulder. "Lisa, I was wondering if . . . well, I want to go for a walk. I need to get some exercise. I was wondering if you'd like to go with me?"

Still feeling nervous about being watched, Lisa wanted to stay close to the group, but Ashley's sincere tone struck her. She put her hand on Ashley's arm. "I'd love to go. Give me just a minute." At the truck, she retrieved her gloves and knit hat.

Sam walked up behind her and wrapped his arms around her.

She relaxed and leaned back against him. Closing her eyes, she basked in the contentment and relief of being held by someone special again.

From the other side of the truck, Ashley called out, "Lisa, are you almost ready?"

Lisa opened her eyes, the precious moment broken.

"She'll be right there," Sam hollered back. He turned Lisa around and looked into her eyes. "You two be careful, and don't be gone too long, okay?" He kissed her lips. "I'd hate to lose either one of you."

"I promise. We'll only be gone for a little while, and we won't go too far." She gave him another quick kiss and slipped out of his arms.

As she walked away, she shivered and glanced around once more to see if anyone was watching her. *This is crazy. What's wrong with me?* She tried to force the discomfort out of her mind by thinking about enjoying her time with Ashley. Unable to shake the feeling of impending doom, she pulled her coat up around her neck and joined Ashley for their walk.

* * *

Large snowflakes fell as Lisa and Ashley walked along the muddy pathways, winding among the hodge-podge of campers, motor homes, and tents scattered haphazardly across the lakebed. Lisa mentally compared this camp to the one in Colorado. She decided the people here looked defeated and run down, whereas in Colorado, they had looked more rebellious and unruly. She kept an eye out for landmarks so that she would be able to make her way safely back to the campsite.

As she and Ashley rounded a corner, Lisa noticed a large group of people standing in line at the rear of a semi-truck trailer. She nudged Ashley forward to see what was going on. They wandered close enough to see soldiers handing out packets of food. She wondered if the government had instilled martial law and were forcibly collecting food and weapons like they had in Colorado. "Come on," she said, turning away from the food line. "I've seen enough."

"Me, too," Ashley said, pulling her coat tighter.

Suddenly, Lisa stopped in her tracks. A familiar black Cadillac was hooked up to a run-down trailer house. "No, it can't be," she murmured, thinking back to the day on the ranch when she'd shot Clem in the leg and forced him to leave her property. Part of her wanted to run, while another part wanted to know for sure.

She stepped to the rear of the car and checked the license plate. When she saw *Wyoming.* a chill ran down her spine. Fearing it might be Clem's car, she decided not to wait around. Grabbing Ashley's arm, she hurried through the campers to make her way back to their own campsite.

The snowflakes grew larger. The bitter wind made her eyes water. Before they had made it halfway back to camp, the snow fell so hard, it covered the ground in a thick layer of white, disturbed only by footprints from people hurrying to their shelters.

"Are you sure this is the way?" Ashley asked. "I don't recognize any of these campers."

"I'm pretty sure this is the right way." *At least, I hope it is.* She struggled through the slippery mud under the snow. The wind swirled around her, changing directions, making it hard for her to keep her bearings. Finally, she stopped and turned around, scanning the vehicles and RVs.

"What are you doing?" Ashley said in a frightened tone as she snuggled up next to Lisa with her hands in her pocket and her teeth chattering. Her cheeks burned red from the icy wind and snow.

"Things look different from different angles. I'm trying to see if I recognize any campers from this direction. I think . . . "

A shadowy figure, wearing a cowboy hat and walking with a limp, emerged out of the swirling snow and grabbed Lisa by the arm of her coat. "What were ya doin' snoopin' 'round my car?"

Lisa froze in place, confused for a moment at the sight of the man's familiar blood-shot eyes. Shocked to see Clem standing before her, her stomach tightened with dread.

"Well, well, well . . . if it ain't the bitch who done shot me in the leg." He clung tightly to her coat as the alcohol on his foul breath hit her between the eyes.

She fought to pull away, but Clem grabbed her other arm to restrain her. As she struggled, she mustered up the courage to bark, "That's right. And if you don't let me go, I'll shoot you again."

He laughed in her face. "Not this time, bitch. No, this time, I'm gonna make you pay good for shootin' me." His face turned hard as he glared at her and breathed down on her. "I bet ya didn't know one of them pellets hit a main nerve, causin' me to lose partial use of my leg . . . did ya?"

Ashley stood next to Lisa with a mask of fear on her pale face. "Lisa, who is this man?" Her frightened eyes moved back and forth between Lisa and Clem.

Fearing for Ashley's welfare, Lisa quit struggling against Clem and forced a calmer tone. "Nobody. Go back to camp. I'll handle this," she said hoping Clem would let Ashley go.

Clem released Lisa with one hand and grabbed Ashley by her long, blond hair.

"Let me go," Ashley screamed, pulling away from him

and trying to loosen his grip from her hair.

Frantic to protect Ashley, Lisa swung her foot toward Clem's crotch.

Seeing the move, Clem turned his hips, catching the blow on his thigh. "You'll have ta do better than that," he sneered. He yanked Ashley off her feet and pulled them across the snow-covered ground.

Ashley screamed as Clem dragged her by the hair.

Lisa stumbled, her arm being pulled faster than her body could keep up on the slick ground.

Clem's black Cadillac and trailer appeared out of the swirling snow.

Stopping suddenly, Clem yanked on Lisa's arm, knocking her to her knees. He swung out his right leg, his cowboy boot catching her above the left ear.

With the stinging cold, stars erupted before her eyes. She shook her head and struggled to stay conscious as she worried about Ashley.

Taking advantage of Clem's distraction, Ashley lunged forward and slammed into Clem, knocking him off balance.

Lisa grabbed his left foot and yanked upward, but he didn't fall like she had hoped.

He laughed. "Whooee, aint this fun? Just wait till we get inside." He kicked Lisa in the side.

Her breath exploded out of her lungs. She felt one of her ribs break.

Ashley screamed and hit Clem in the face. Her gloves, softening the blows, didn't seem to affect him.

He backhanded her with his right hand, knocking her into the snow at his boots. He opened the trailer door, bent over, and grabbed Ashley's arm. Yanking her to her feet, he shoved her into the trailer.

Determined to keep Clem from hurting Ashley, Lisa struggled to get up.

"Oh, no, ya don't," Clem snarled as he slammed his fist into her face, knocking her down again.

Lisa fell helplessly into the snow. As darkness began to overtake her, Lisa thought about Ashley, how she had failed to protect her, how Sam would blame her for Clem's actions, and how she would lose everything wonderful that she had gained.

* * *

Sam, sitting cross-legged on his sleeping bag, worried about Lisa and Ashley. They had been gone far too long, especially after the wind had picked up and the snow had begun to fall harder. "I'm going to go see if I can find them," he said to Dave, curled up in his sleeping bag.

"Do you want me to come with you?"

"No, I'll get John to go." Sam pulled on his coat, hat, and gloves. Reaching under his pillow, he removed his gun and slipped it into the right pocket of his coat.

"Be careful, Dad."

Sam nodded.

Outside, the wind swirled the snow, reducing visibility to less than a hundred feet.

"I had a feeling you'd go looking for them," John said as he stepped out of the other tent.

"And I suppose you're going with me?"

"I wouldn't miss it."

Trudging through the three inches of snow now covering the alkali flats, Sam and John wove their way through the trailers, motor homes, and tents while calling out for Lisa and Ashley.

A man in dirty jeans and a stained t-shirt threw open the door of a shabby trailer. "What the hell's all the yellin' 'bout?" he slurred, waving a half-empty whiskey bottle.

"We're looking for two missing women," Sam said over the wind. "Have you . . ."

The drunk cut him off. "I ain't seed nobody, so quit yer yellin' and leave me 'lone, or I'll come over there and kick yer ass." He stumbled down the two rickety steps. "In fact, I'm gonna kick yer ass anyway." He sat his bottle in the snow and swaggered towards Sam and John.

Infuriated at the drunk for delaying his search, Sam pulled his gun out and pointed it at the man's face.

The drunk slid to a stop and put his hands up.

Sam growled, "Go back inside and leave us alone."

Wide-eyed, the man said, "I didn't mean no harm." He walked backwards. "I wuz just kiddin' 'round. No hard feelin's." He fumbled with the door handle. When it finally opened, he hurried inside and slammed the door.

A scream rose out of the swirling snow.

"Ashley!" Sam shouted. With John hot on his heels, he ran through the campground in the direction of the scream.

Sam saw a black Cadillac and an old trailer. He caught sight of Ashley being shoved through the trailer door by a man in a cowboy hat. He glanced at the figure lying on the ground and instantly knew it was Lisa. *Son-of-a-bitch! It's Clem.* In a rage, he charged. He slammed into the man and bounced him off of the trailer.

The man reeled and staggered on the slippery snow, coming to a stop at the trunk of the black Cadillac. "What the hell ya doin?" he said, eyeing Sam warily.

By this time, John had an arm around Ashley and stopped to help Lisa get up.

Sam glared. "I'll bet you're Clem, aren't you?"

"How'd ya know that?"

"The black Cadillac, plus, Lisa told me all about you." Sam slowly moved toward him, ready to teach him a lesson.

"She's a lying little bitch and . . . "

Sam swung his leg, catching Clem in the crotch.

Clem doubled over.

Sam put all his might into a right fist, hitting Clem on his chin.

Clem fell on the trunk of the car and slid to the ground.

Sam grabbed Clem by the front of his coat. Feeling a sharp pain from the injury to his left arm, Sam lifted Clem only far enough to get right into his face. "If you ever bother or harass Lisa or my daughter again, I'll hunt you down and shoot you in both knees. Do you understand what I'm saying?"

Clem's bloodshot eyes blinked a few times. He nodded as he wiped the blood from his mouth.

Sam threw the man down and left him lying on the ground. He turned to Lisa, leaning against John. Ashley stood on the other side of Lisa and stared at Clem with a smirk of satisfaction. Sam took Lisa into his arms. "How're you feeling?"

"A little groggy."

"Can you walk?"

She pulled her head back and nodded.

Sam bent down and kissed her lips. "Come on, let's go back to camp."

As they walked back to camp, the snow stopped falling. The clouds cleared and Sam saw stars appearing in the sky. He sighed with relief that the storm had ended. That meant they would be able to get on the road in the morning. If they could just get to Jerry's place in Medford, they would finally be able to settle down and start rebuilding their lives. With all the problems they had faced since leaving Wyoming, Sam just wanted everything to stop, to get back to normal. He was tired of worrying about everyone in his party being killed.

He pulled Lisa a little closer as they trudged through the muddy snow. *I lost Linda in Casper when things went haywire. I just can't lose Lisa . . . nor the kids. We've just got to make it a little further. Just a little further.*

Chapter 22

When they got to the little town of Weed, Sam called Jerry. "Hey, brother, we're going through Weed now, so we should be there in what, about an hour?"

"I'm glad you called, Sam, we've got a problem up here."

Sam's heart sank. He was so close to getting his family to safety and, now, he was sure Jerry was going to tell him they wouldn't be able to stay in the area. "What's wrong?"

"A group of Arian Nation skinheads have been attacking small groups of travelers in the area and burning homes. Last night, they went too far."

Sam was relieved Jerry wasn't going to turn them away, but now he was concerned there might be another dangerous situation looming in the near future for him and his party. "What did they do?" Sam asked, not really wanting to know.

"They stopped five vehicles and killed twenty people."

Sam swallowed hard. He feared they might end up with another battle on their hands, like in Barstow. "How many of these skinheads are there?"

"We're not sure, ten . . . maybe twelve."

"Do you think we'll run into them before we get to Medford?" Sam asked. He tried to convince himself that he and his companions wouldn't have any problems and, if they did, they would be able to handle it. There were hundreds of square miles in this area. What chance was there that they would run into this gang? Still, in the back of his mind, he cringed at the thought of having to face another battle.

"We've gotten together a group of people, and we're trying to find them," Jerry said, "but so far, we haven't had much luck. You may want to stop where you're at until we get this situation under control."

Lisa mouthed, "What?"

"Let me talk to Lisa and the kids. I'll call you back." He hung up and pulled over. "Let's get out and wait for the others."

Lisa's blue eyes flashed a worried look, but she said nothing as she got out of the passenger's seat and made her way to a clearing under a large pine tree just off the side of the road.

Dave and Ashley, both bundled in their coats, opened their doors and made their way to Lisa.

Although the sky remained clear, a sharp wind cut through Sam's open coat as he motioned to the others to get out of their vehicles and join him. He wanted to go on, but to be fair to the others, he needed to make sure they would agree to it.

When everyone had gathered near his truck, Sam sighed and started into his explanation. "My brother said there are some skinheads in the area that are burning houses and killing people."

Jean moaned and grabbed Richard's arm. Her face seemed tired and old, as though she couldn't face one more disaster.

Richard drew her close. "What do you propose we do?" he said to Sam.

Sam said, "The way I see it, we've got three options. We can camp out here until Jerry and his friends catch these skinheads, but who's to say the skinheads won't find us here? We could turn back, but we won't be any safer than we've been in the past. Our other option is to try to get to Medford."

John looked at Sunshine. After getting a hesitant, confirming nod from her, he announced, "Sunshine and I will go on with you."

Jean stepped forward. "Are you sure you want to go into this kind of situation with an Indian and two black people?"

John put his hand on Sam's shoulder. "Jean is right. Maybe you, Lisa, and the kids should go ahead. Once the situation settles down, the rest of us will come up and join you."

Sam shook his head. "You're my friends. I'm not going to leave you behind. We're all in this together."

He looked at Dave, Ashley, and Lisa. He wouldn't feel completely at ease until he had them at his brother's home and safe. "I think we can make it to my brother's. I'd like to try. I don't want to force anybody to continue." He looked at his kids, hoping he was making the right decision. He shrugged, trying to lighten the tension. "And besides, what are the chances that we'll run into these guys anyway?" "

"I agree, Dad," Ashley said. "I'm tired of running and fighting and worrying all the time. I just want to get to Uncle Jerry's, where we can be safe again. If that means having one last fight with a group of skinheads, then I say, let's go and get it over with."

"I'm all for going," Lisa said, stepping forward.

"What about you, Dave?" Sam asked.

"We've faced a volcano, unruly mobs, and we've lost Mom." He paused for a moment while he looked from Sam to Ashley and back again. "We've been trapped behind enemy lines and been attacked by a gang in the race war. If these skinheads know what's good for them, they'll watch out, because we're going to Oregon."

Pride for his son and daughter flooded through Sam. "Okay," he said with a lump in his throat. "I'll call Jerry and tell him we're on our way."

* * *

Five miles past the California/Oregon state line, Sam drove around a corner and saw a roadblock. Ten or twelve cars and trucks, parked on the freeway, blocked it completely. Five skinheads popped up from behind the cars.

As Sam slowed to a near-stop, a cold sweat beaded his forehead. *This can't be happening.* A tremor passed through his body. *We should've waited in Weed. What was I thinking? How could I have brought Dave, Ashley and Lisa into another life-threatening situation?* As John and Richard stopped behind him, Sam thought to gun the engine and turn around, but five cars suddenly pull up behind them, blocking their exit.

Six more skinheads got out of the vehicles.

Sam nearly peed in his pants. He realized the gang had picked a good spot. The freeway passed through a cut in the mountains at this point. There would be no way to escape. He nervously glanced back at the kids.

They held their guns with solemn faces, looking to him for guidance.

Lisa gripped her shotgun in her lap and pensively looked ahead.

Waiting for John's signal to make a move, Sam wiped his sweaty hands on his pants. He noticed the calmness in his hand and idly wondered, *Is that good or bad?*

John's head turned from the skinheads in the front to the menacing group walking toward them from the back.

Eight against eleven, Sam thought as everything seemed to move in slow motion. *Not good odds, given the fact that Sunshine and Jean won't pick up a gun and Ashley probably won't hit anybody. That's five to eleven.*

He briefly closed his eyes and steeled himself. He thought of how Linda had died needlessly. He couldn't let that happen to his family now. He *wasn't* going to let that happen. He had come too far to let some bastards take away all that he had left in his life. If someone was going to threaten his family now, he was going to go out fighting to the end. A sudden burst of energy surged through him as his eyes opened and he caught the tail of John's signal.

Dave, Ashley, and Lisa threw their doors open and jumped out screaming at the top of their lungs. They shot at the five bald, white heads coming from the roadblock.

Caught off-guard, three men went down.

Sam scrambled to get out of the car as the two remaining skinheads scurried behind their vehicles. As they returned fire, Lisa, Dave, and Ashley dove into the truck for cover.

"Get down, Dad," Ashley screamed.

Enraged at the bastards, Sam ignored Ashley and stood out in the open with his gun in hand.

One of the skinheads popped up and fired a couple of wild shots, both ricocheting off the pavement. The man disappeared behind the car again.

The other skinhead performed the same action a few seconds later.

Anticipating a repeat from the first skinhead, Sam aimed carefully. When the bald head came up, Sam fired, hitting the man between the eyes before he got off a shot.

The second skinhead, screaming in anger, popped up with his gun.

Pow. Sam's bullet took him down.

Sam spun around to help John and Richard, but the dead bodies of the other six skinheads lay sprawled across the highway.

Lowering his gun, Sam let out a deep breath. *It's over.*

As Lisa and the kids got out of the truck, Sam heard vehicles coming down the freeway from the other side of the roadblock. He yelled, "Get back in the truck. More are coming. Stay hidden and be ready to shoot." He stood behind the driver's door and waited for a better view of the vehicles.

A parade of Jeeps, trucks, and cars pulled up to the roadblock. A tall, stocky man with gray hair and a pot belly jumped out of the lead Jeep.

Sam's shoulders slumped and he let out a deep sigh.

The man made his way through the parked cars and stopped in front of Sam. "It's good to see you, little brother." Jerry held out his hand.

"It's good to see you, too." Sam took Jerry's hand and shook it vigorously.

"You don't seem to need our help," said a portly, bald man wearing a rumpled suit. When Sam glanced at this running shoes, the man said, "I didn't have time to change out of my suit, so I just slipped on my running shoes and grabbed my gun." He grinned and shrugged his shoulders.

"Sam," Jerry said, "this is Oscar Portman, the mayor of Medford."

"It's nice to meet you, Oscar," Sam said, shaking his hand. "I'd like to introduce you to my friends."

Lisa said her hello's and moved off to the side while Ashley greeted her uncle.

Lisa and Ashley looked a little pale, and Sam knew that the killings had been hard on them. He made a promise to himself to never put them in a situation where they would have to kill again.

Dave looked calm.

Sam felt relieved to see he wasn't thriving on the adrenaline of action anymore.

John and Richard shook hands with Jerry and Oscar

while Sunshine and Jean remained in the vehicles.

"Our women are a little unnerved, right now," Richard explained. "They'll meet you a little later, when things settled down."

Oscar nodded sympathetically. After he instructed the other members of the group from town to start cleaning up the bodies and moving the cars from the freeway, he stepped toward Sam. "You and your friends are welcome to stay in Medford as long as you want. We're always looking for good solid citizens and, after what Jerry told me about your trip, and with the obvious battle you just won here, you're just what we need."

"Thank you, Oscar," Sam said with deep appreciation. "You don't know how much that means to me and to all of us. It would be good to have a place called home again."

* * *

Sam followed Jerry into town. They stopped in front of a white house with a white picket fence around the yard. Jerry's wife Sandy came out onto the porch and waved to Jerry, obviously relieved her husband had made it home safely.

A sense of relief flowed through Sam as he turned off the ignition. He could finally relax and let his guard down. *It's over. It's finally over. The kids, Lisa, me . . . we all made it safely. Thank God.* He closed his eyes and took a deep breath, slowly letting it out. He felt Lisa take hold of his hand. He opened his eyes and smiled at her. *Then again, some things are just beginning.* He turned to the kids. "Why don't you two go see your Aunt Sandy. Lisa and I need a moment alone."

As the kids got out of the truck, Lisa turned to face him.

He reached out and took her hands. Looking into her sparkling blue eyes, he said, "Maybe all of this was meant to happen so we would end up together. Whatever the reason, I'm glad we found each other. I don't know what the future holds for us, but with you by my side, I feel like I can accomplish anything."

Lisa responded with a warm, loving smile.

Epilogue
Six months later

"Honey, telephone," Lisa hollered to Sam.

He sat in his recliner watching the evening news. He muted the T.V. "Who is it?" he asked as she walked into the room.

"It's John." She handed him the phone and sat down on the edge of his chair.

"Hey, buddy," Sam said, "how's the weather in Arizona?"

"Warm and wonderful. How's the weather in Oregon?"

"Cold and crappy. It's been raining nonstop for a month."

"Yeah, well, I tried to convince you to come back to Arizona with us, but *no*, you wanted to stay in Oregon."

"I'd rather deal with our rain than your heat," Sam retorted.

"Even though you're only a hundred miles from a volcano?" John asked.

"A *dormant* volcano," Sam clarified.

Suddenly, Sam noticed the house shaking. He didn't hear what John was saying as he stared at the T.V. He dropped the phone and turned up the volume.

"Mt. Shasta," the announcer said breathlessly, "which has been dormant for over two hundred years . . . just exploded."

Finding a baby Triceratops in the house, sixteen-year-old Jeff Watson confronts his two brothers, Riley and Wayne, who claim to have gone back in time and accidently brought the dinosaur home. Jeff's friend, Mitch Arnoldson, buys their story, but Jeff can't believe Riley built a real, working time machine with his computer. Playing along, Jeff agrees to pack a bag and make the trip through time to take the dinosaur home. Carlita and Macy, the girlfriends of Jeff and Mitch, go along, just for the fun of it.

Much to Jeff's surprise, Riley's time machine really works, and in a flash, Jeff finds himself in a world as alien to him as the moon. Separated from Mitch and the girls, Jeff must keep himself and his brothers alive until they can go home.

A devious man from the government, determined to keep Riley's computer a secret, follows the kids with a plan to steal Riley's computer and leave the kids stranded in the Jurassic Era. Will Jeff and his brothers avoid being eaten by hungry T-Rexes, only to find themselves stuck millions of years in the past? Or will Jeff find a way to get all of them home safely?

Look for this and other books by Layne Walker at
amazon.com and other online stores

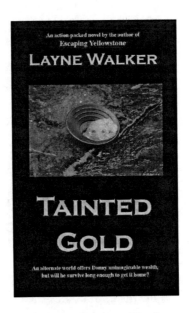

An action-packed novel by the author of
Escaping Yellowstone

LAYNE WALKER

TAINTED

GOLD

An alternate world offers Donny unimaginable wealth,
but will he survive long enough to get it home?

Unimaginable Wealth,
Unimaginable Beauty,
Unimaginable Danger.

When Donny Jamison discovers a portal to an alternate world, he quickly realizes the financial possibilities and enlists the help of his brother, Eric. They put together a team of ten other people and, with the aid of the other-world natives, set off on a quest to gather all the gold they can find. But problems soon arise. Donny has to contend with an angry native who thinks the portal and everyone who comes through it is evil. Donny finds a world that's more dangerous and unforgiving than he'd ever imagined. One of the members of his group gets drunk and is accused of killing a young native girl. Will Donny and his group die violent, horrible deaths at the hands of bloodthirsty natives? Or will they make it through the portal and back to their world and safety?

Look for this and other books by Layne Walker
at amazon.com and other online stores

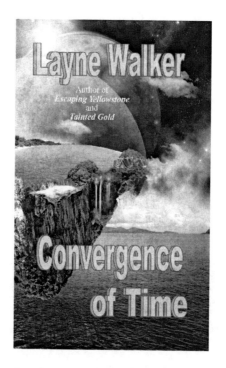

Exploring the desert to avoid family guests, Gavin Clark steps into an invisible web and finds himself caught in a world where time and space are compressed. Dinosaurs and other dangerous creatures of past eras roam parts of the land. Groups of Earth's people from the past, present, and future come together in a melting pot of humanity, thrown into a new world without the advantages of modern technology and the comforts of their former communities. People age at a very slow rate. No children are born. And more importantly, no one has found a way out. Will Gavin find the key to escaping this world to be home with his wife and children again? Journey with him through a maze of peculiar people, shocking circumstances, and unpredictable events as he sets on out a quest to find the answers to getting home.

Layne Walker lives in Lake Havasu City, AZ, where he enjoys exploring the desert, dancing, and writing. He began his writing career in the summer of 2010 when he was challenged to write his own novel after years of being an avid novel reader. Once the writing fever got hold of him, he found himself on the adventure of his own life, constantly filled with new ideas for more novels, more action, more fun, and more surprises yet to come. To find out more, visit his website at www.laynewalkerbooks.com.

CPSIA information can be obtained at www.ICGtesting.com
Printed in the USA
LVOW06s1936260514

387300LV00034B/1730/P